NEW YORK'S FINEST REBEL

BY

TRISH WYLIE

MILLS
BOON®

First published in Great Britain 2012
by Mills & Boon, an imprint of Harlequin (UK) Limited.
Large Print edition 2012
Harlequin (UK) Limited, Eton House,
18-24 Paradise Road, Richmond, Surrey TW9 1SR

© Trish Wylie 2012

ISBN: 978 0 263 22603 4

Printed and bound in Great Britain
by CPI Antony Rowe, Chippenham, Wiltshire

To my lovely editor Flo, fellow member
of the 'I heart Daniel Brannigan' fanclub.

CHAPTER ONE

'Every girl knows there are days for heels and days for flats. It could be a metaphor for life if you think about it. Let's all make today a heels day, shall we?'

SIREN red and dangerously high, they were the sexiest pair of heels Daniel Brannigan had ever seen. Silently cursing the amount of time it took to haul the cage doors into place, he watched them disappear upstairs.

He *really* wanted to meet the woman in those shoes.

Punching on the button until there was a jerk of upward movement, he tried to play catch-up in the slowest elevator ever invented. After the first of three endlessly monotonous trips, he knew the stairs were going to be his preferred mode of travel in the future. But until he had all of his worldly possessions—few that they were—carted from his truck to the fifth floor, he didn't have a choice.

A flash of red appeared in his peripheral vision. *Target acquired.*

Turning in the small space, he assessed each detail as it came into sight. Thin straps circled dainty ankles, the angle of her small feet adding enough shape to her calves to remind him that he was overdue for some R & R. If she lived in the same apartment block he was moving into, it was a complication he could do without. But if the effect her shoes had on his libido was anything to go by, he reckoned it was worth the risk. He hadn't earned the nickname Danger Danny for nothing.

The elevator jarred to an unexpected halt, an elderly woman with a small dog in her arms scowling pointedly at the boxes piled around his feet. 'Going down?'

'Up,' he replied curtly. Rocking forward, he nudged the button with his elbow.

Don't disappear on me, babe.

The adrenalin rush of pursuit had always done it for him, as had the kind of woman it took to wear a skirt so short it made him stifle a groan when it came into view. Flared at mid-smooth-skinned-thigh, the flirty cheerleader number lovingly hugged the curve of her hips before dipping in at a narrow waist. He glanced at the fine-boned hand curled around handles of bags labelled with names that meant nothing to him, mouth curving into a smile at the lack of anything sparkling on her ring finger. On the floor below his, she turned to speak to someone in the hall. To his frustration it meant he couldn't see her face as the elevator creaked by. Instead he was left with an image of tumbling locks of long dark hair and the sound of sparkling feminine laughter.

Fighting with the cage again when the elevator stopped, he did what he had done on his previous trips and nudged a box forward to fill the gap. In the following moment of silence, footsteps sounded on the stairs. A trickle of awareness ran down his spine as he turned, gaze rising until he was looking into large dark eyes. Eyes that narrowed as his smile faded.

'Jorja,' he said dryly.

'Daniel,' she replied in the same tone before she tilted her head and arched a brow. 'Didn't occur to you anyone else might want to use the elevator today?'

'Stairs are good for cardio.'

'That would be a no, then.'

'Offering to help me move in? That's neigh-bourly of you.' He thrust the box in his arms at her, letting go before she had an opportunity to refuse.

There was a tinkle of breaking glass as it hit the floor between their feet.

'Oops.' She blinked.

Oops, his ass. The fact she'd obviously made interesting changes in wardrobe while he was overseas didn't make her any less irritating than she'd been for the last five and a half years. 'No welcome-home banner?' he asked.

'Wouldn't that suggest I'm happy you're here?'

'You got a problem with me being here, you should have made it known when my application came up in front of the residents committee.'

'What makes you think I didn't?'

'Clue was in the words unanimous decision.' He shrugged. 'What can I say? People like when a cop lives in the building. Makes them feel secure.'

She smiled a saccharine-sweet smile. 'The elderly woman you ticked off two floors down is the head of the residents' committee. I give it a week before she starts a petition to have you evicted.'

Daniel took a measured breath. He had never met another woman who had the same effect on his nerves as fingernails down a chalkboard. 'Know your biggest problem, babe?'

'Don't call me babe.'

'You underestimate my ability to be adorable when I set my mind to it. I can have the poodle lady baking cookies for me inside forty-eight hours.'

'Bichon.'

'What?'

'The dog. It's a Bichon frise.'

'It got a name?'

'Gershwin.' She rolled her eyes when she realized what she was doing. 'And I'm afraid that's my quota for helpfulness all used up for the day.'

Bending over, he lifted the box at their feet, held it to his ear and gave it a brisk shake. 'You owe me a half-dozen glasses.'

'Sue me,' she said as she turned on her heel.

As he followed her down the hall Daniel's errant gaze lowered to watch the sway of her hips before he reminded himself who he was looking at. He had done some dumb things in his time but checking out Jorja Dawson was stupid on a whole new level. If she were the last woman left in the state of New York, he would take a vow of celibacy before getting involved with her. He even had a list of reasons why.

Casually tossing long locks of shining hair over her shoulder, she reached into her purse and turned to face him at the door to her apartment. 'I don't suppose you're considering showing your face at Sunday lunch once you've unpacked? Your mother would appreciate it.'

Number six on his list: *Family involvement.*

He looked into her eyes. 'Will you be there?'

'Never miss it.'

'Tell them I said hi.'

'Are you saying you don't go because I'm there?'

'Don't flatter yourself.' He moved the box in his arms to dig into a pocket for his key. 'If I rearranged my life around you I wouldn't be moving into an apartment across the hall from you. But just so you know—' he leaned closer and lowered his voice '—you'll move before I do.'

'You've never stayed anywhere longer than six months,' she stated categorically. 'And even then it was because the army sent you there.'

'Navy,' he corrected without missing a beat. 'And if there's one thing you should keep in mind about the Marines, it's that we don't give up ground.'

'I've lived here for more than four years. I'm not going anywhere.'

'Then I guess we'll be seeing a lot of each other.'

Something he could have done without, frankly. Not that he was likely to tell her, but she was the main reason he'd debated taking the apartment. She was a spy who could report back to the rest of the Brannigan clan in weekly discussions over a roast and cheesecake from Junior's. But as far as Daniel was concerned, if his family wanted to know how he was doing they could ask. When they did, he'd give them the same answer he had for the last eight years. With a few more recent additions to throw them off the trail.

He was fine, thanks. Sure it was good to be home. No, he hadn't had any problems settling back into his unit. Yes, if the Reserves called him up again he would go.

They didn't need to know more than that.

'You know *your* problem, Daniel?' She angled her head to the irritating angle she did best. 'You think your being here bugs me when to be honest I couldn't care less where you are, what you're doing or who you're doing it with.'

'Is that so?'

'Mmm-hmm.' She nodded. 'I'm not one of those

women you can turn into a gibbering idiot with a smile. I just hope your ego can handle that.'

'Careful, Jo, I might take that as a challenge.'

There was a low burst of the same sparkling laughter he heard on the stairwell, making him wonder why it was he hadn't recognized it before. Most likely it was because she didn't laugh much when he was around. The second it looked as if she would, he'd say something to ruin her mood. He'd been good at that long before he'd started to put any effort into it.

'I had no idea you had a sense of humour,' she said with enough derogatory amusement to tempt him to rise to the bait.

Before he could, she opened the door to her apartment and stepped over the threshold. She turned, her gaze sliding over his body from head to toe and back up again; her laughter louder as she swung the door shut.

Daniel shook his head. *Damn, she bugged him.*

Damn, he bugged her.

Leaning back against the door, Jo took a long breath and frowned at the fact her heart rate was running a little faster than usual. If taking the stairs in heels had that much of an effect, she might have to consider taking a gym membership.

Granted, a small part of it could probably be chalked up to frustration at her inability to hold a conversation with him without it turning into a verbal sparring match. But she hadn't been sparring alone. To say they brought out the worst in each other would be the understatement of the century.

Heading across the open-plan living area to her bedroom, she resisted the urge to hunt out fluffy slippers and a pair of pyjamas. If he drove her into ice-cream-eating attire on his first day there wasn't a hope she could survive the next three months. When her cell phone rang an hour later, she checked the name on the screen before answering.

'I still can't believe you've done this to me.'

A smile sounded in Olivia's voice. 'Which part? Moving out, putting you in a bridesmaid dress or telling Danny about the apartment next door?'

'I think you know what I mean,' Jo smirked sarcastically. 'I need a new BFF; my ideal man could have moved into that apartment if you hadn't mentioned it to Mr Personality.'

'Since when have you been looking for an ideal

man? And anyway, he won't be there long. Short lease, remember?'

'If he renews I'm making a little doll and sticking dozens of pins in it.' Leaving the mirror where she had been staging a personal fashion show in front of hyper-critical eyes, she headed for the kitchen. 'But just so you know, he's determined I'll move first.'

Since everyone who had ever lived in Manhattan knew what their apartment meant to a New Yorker, she didn't have to explain how ridiculous it was for Daniel to think she was going anywhere. The apartment she'd shared with Olivia—and from time to time still did with Jess—was a few hundred square feet of space she could call her own.

She hadn't worked her butt off to end up back in a place she'd sworn she would never find herself again.

'You saw him already? Is there blood in the hall?'

'Not yet. But give it a few weeks and only one of us is leaving this building intact.' Lifting the empty coffeepot, she sighed at the heavy beat coming from across the hall. 'Can you hear that?'

She held the phone out at arm's length for a moment.

'My brother and classic rock go together like—'

'Satan and eternal torture?' Jo enquired.

'Probably not the best time to mention he's agreed to be in the wedding party, is it?'

'I am *not* walking up the aisle with him.'

'You can have Tyler.'

Good call. She loved Tyler Brannigan. *He* was fun to be around. 'I thought he was determined he wasn't wearing a monkey suit. How did you talk him into it?'

'Danny? The same way we got him to his niece's birthday party last month. Only this time Blake helped...'

Meaning he'd lost a bet. Jo smiled a small smile at the idea of Liv's new fiancé tag-teaming with the rest of the Brannigan brothers against one of their own on poker night. She spooned coffee granules into the percolator. *Go Blake.*

'How did he look to you?'

The question made Jo blink, her voice threaded with suspicion. 'Same as he always looks. Why?'

'I take it you haven't watched the news today.'

'No.' She stepped into the living room and pointed the remote at the TV screen. 'What did I miss?'

'Wait for it...'

The report appeared almost instantaneously on the local news channel. Unable to hear what was said without racking the volume up to competitive levels, she read the feed across the bottom of the screen. It mentioned a yet-to-be-named Emergency Services Officer who might or might not have unhooked his safety harness to rescue a man on the Williamsburg Bridge. If it was who she thought it was Jo could have told them the answer. The camera attempted to focus on a speck of arm-waving humanity among the suspension cables at the exact moment another speck closed in on him. For a second they came dangerously close to falling; a collective gasp coming from the crowd of gawkers on the ground. At the last minute several more specks surrounded them and hauled them to safety.

A round of applause sounded on the screen as Jo shook her head. 'You got to be kidding me.'

'I know.' Olivia sighed. 'Mom is climbing the walls. It was tough enough for her when he was overseas…'

'Did you call him?'

'He's not picking up.'

Jo glared at the door. 'I'll call you back.'

In the hall, she banged her fist several times

against wood before the music lowered and the door opened.

'Call your mother,' she demanded as she thrust her cell phone at him.

'What's wrong?'

Ignoring what could have almost been mistaken for concern in his deep voice, she turned her hand around, hit speed-dial and lifted the phone to her ear.

'You're an inconsiderate asshat,' she muttered.

The second his mother picked up she thrust the phone at him again, snatching her hand back when warm fingers brushed against hers.

'No, it's me. I'm fine. Someone would have called you if I wasn't. You know that.' He took a step back and closed the door in Jo's face.

Back in her apartment, she froze and swore under her breath at the fact he had her cell phone. Her life was in that little rectangle of technology. Hadn't stopped to think that one through, had she? Marching back to the kitchen, she lifted the apartment phone, checked the Post-it note on the crowded refrigerator door and dialled his sister's new number.

'He's talking to your mother now.'

'What did you do?' Liv asked.

'Told him exactly what I thought of him.'

'To his face?'

Picking up where she'd left off, Jo hit the switch on the percolator. 'I've never had a problem saying what I think to his face. You *know* that.'

There was a firm knock against wood.

'Hang on.' When she opened the door and her gaze met narrowed blue eyes, she took the phone from him, replacing it with the one in her hand. 'Your sister.'

Lifting the receiver to his ear, he stepped across the threshold. 'Hey, sis, what's up?'

Jo blinked. How had he ended up in her apartment? Swinging the door shut, she turned and went back to the kitchen. If he thought it was becoming a regular occurrence, he could forget it. She wanted to spend time with him as much as she loved the idea of having her fingernails pulled out. Glancing briefly at the room that seemed smaller with him in it, she frowned when he looked at her from the corner of his eye.

His gaze swept over her body, lingering for longer than necessary on her feet. What was *that*?

Jo resisted the urge to look down at what she was wearing. There was nothing wrong with her outfit. If anything, it covered more than the one she was wearing last time he saw her. Personally she loved how the high-waist black pants made her legs seem longer, especially when accompanied by a pair of deep purple, skyscraper-heeled Louboutins. Five feet six inches didn't exactly make her small. But considering the number of models towering over her like Amazons on regular occasions during working hours, she appreciated every additional illusionary inch of height. She shook her head a minute amount. Why should she care what he thought? What he knew about fashion wouldn't fill a thimble. His jeans were a prime example.

Judging by the way they were worn at the knees and around the pockets on his—

She sharply averted her gaze. If he caught her looking at his rear she would never hear the end of it.

The man already had an ego the size of Texas.

'It's my job,' he said with a note of impatience as he paced around the room. 'The line didn't reach... There wasn't time... I knew they had my back. You done, 'cos I'm pretty sure your friend has three more calls to make...'

Unrepentant, Jo grabbed her favourite mug and set it on the counter. She hoped Liv gave him hell, especially when he had just confirmed his stupid-ity. What kind of idiot unhooked his safety har-ness that high up? Hadn't he heard of a little thing called gravity?

Turning as the coffee bubbled, she leaned her hip against the counter and folded her arms, study-ing him while he paced. His jaw tensed, broad chest lifting and lowering beneath a faded Giants T-Shirt. He looked…weary? No, weary wasn't the right word. Tired, maybe—as if he hadn't slept much lately. Not that she cared about that either, but since Liv asked how he looked, apparently she felt the need to study him more closely than usual and once she'd gotten started…

Okay, so if injected with a truth serum she sup-posed she would admit there were understandable reasons women tended to trip over their feet when he smiled. Vivid blue eyes, shortly cropped dark blond hair, the hint of shadow on his strong jaw… Add them to the ease with which his long, lean, muscular frame covered the ground and there wasn't a single gal in Manhattan who wouldn't volunteer their phone number.

Not that they'd hold his interest for long.

'Well, you can stop. I'm fine. Don't you have

a wedding to plan? Said I would, didn't I?' His
gaze slid across the room. 'She'll call you back.'

Before he hung up, Jo was across the apartment
and had swung the door open with a smile. But
instead of his taking the hint, a large hand closed
it, his palm flattening on the wood by her head.
His body loomed over hers. If they'd been outside
he would have blocked out the sun.

'We obviously need to talk,' he said flatly.

No, they didn't. Jo gritted her teeth together,
rapidly losing what was left of her patience. She
was contemplating grinding a stiletto heel into
one of his boots when he took a short breath and
added, 'Butting your pretty little nose into other
people's business might be okay with other folks.
It's not with me.'

'Try answering your phone and I won't have to.'
She arched a brow. 'Is the fact your family might
think you have a death wish so very difficult for
you to grasp?'

'I don't have a death wish.'

'Unhooking your harness is standard procedure,
is it?'

'Go stand on the chair.'

She faltered. 'What?'

'You heard me.'

When she didn't move, he circled her wrist with a thumb and forefinger. The jolt of heat that travelled swiftly up her arm made her drop her chin and frown as he led her across the room. Now he was *touching* her? He never touched her. If anything it had always felt as if there were a quarantine zone around her.

'What do you think you're doing?' she asked.

'Staging a demonstration…'

Her eyes widened when he released her wrist, set his hands on her waist and hoisted her onto an overstuffed chair. 'Where do you get off—? Don't stand on my furniture!'

Feet spread shoulder-width apart on the deep cushions of the sofa, he tested the springs with a couple of small bounces before jerking his chin at her. 'Jump.'

'What?'

'Jump.'

That was it, she'd had enough. She wasn't the remotest bit interested in playing games. What was he—*five*?

But when she attempted to get down off the chair, a long arm snapped around her waist and she was launched into mid-air. The next thing she knew, she was slammed into what felt like a wall of heat, a sharp gasp hauled through her parted lips. She jerked her chin up and stared into his eyes, the tips of their noses almost touching. What. The. Hell?

'You see...' he said in a mesmerizing rumble '...it's all about balance...'

Surreally, his intense gaze examined her face in a way that suggested he'd never looked at her before. But what was more disconcerting was how it felt as if there weren't anywhere they weren't touching. The sensation of her breasts crushed against his chest made it difficult to breathe, the contact sending an erotic jolt through her abdomen. How could she be attracted to him when she disliked him so much?

When she was lowered—unbearably slowly—along the length of his large body, Jo had no choice but to grasp wide shoulders until her feet hit the cushions. She swayed as she let go. For a moment she even felt light-headed.

'I knew what I was doing.' Stepping down, he lifted her onto the floor as if she weighed nothing.

Taking an immediate step back, Jo dropped her arms to her sides. Her gaze lowered to his chest. She should be angry, ticked off beyond belief he had the gall to touch her and—worse still—have an effect on her body. She liked her world right-side-up, *thank you very much*, and if he knew what he had done to her...

Folding her arms over heavy breasts, she lifted her chin again. 'The giant footprints you've left on my sofa make us even for the half-dozen glasses.'

'If you've got nothing better to do with your time than talk about me to my family, try taking up a hobby.'

A small cough of disbelief left her lips. 'I have plenty of things to fill my time.'

'Dating obviously isn't one of them,' he said dryly.

'Meaning *what*, exactly?'

'Meaning I may have forgotten why it is you've stayed single for so long, but after an hour it's starting to come back to me.' He folded his arms in a mirror of her stance. 'Ever consider being nice from time to time might improve the odds of getting laid?'

'Since when has my sex life been remotely in the region of any of your business?'

'If I had to guess, I'd say around about the same time my relationship with my family became yours.'

Reaching for the kind of strength that had got-

ten her through worse things than an argument
in the past, Jo smiled sweetly. 'Try not to let the
door hit your ass on the way out.'

'That's the best you've got?' he asked with a lift
of his brows. 'You're obviously out of practice.'
He nodded firmly. 'Don't worry, we'll soon get
you combat-ready again.'

Jo sighed heavily and headed for the door. She
didn't look at him as he crossed the room. But
for some completely unknown reason, just before
he left, she heard herself ask, 'Don't you ever get
tired of this?'

Where had *that* come from?

Daniel stopped, turned his head and studied her
with an intense gaze. 'Quitting on me, babe?'

She frowned when the softly spoken question
did something weird to her chest. 'Don't call me
babe.'

When he didn't move, the air seemed to thicken
in the space between them. Stupid hormones—
even if she was in the market for a relationship
he was the last man—

'You want to negotiate a truce?'

She didn't know what had possessed her to ask
the question in the first place and now he was asking if she wanted them to be *friends*? She stifled

a burst of laughter. 'Did I give the impression I
was waving a white flag? I'm talking about you,
not me. You look tired, Daniel.' She pouted. 'Is
the energy required pretending to be a nice guy
to everyone else finally wearing you down?'

His eyes darkened. 'Questioning my stamina,
babe?'

The 'babe' thing was really starting to get to
her.

Taking a step closer, he leaned his face close
enough for her to feel the warmth of his breath
on her cheeks.

'Bad idea,' he warned.

Ignoring the flutter of her pulse, Jo stiffened her
spine. Since childhood she'd had a code she lived
by; one she still found hard to break, even for the
tiny handful of people she allowed to occupy an
equally tiny corner of her heart. Show any sign
of weakness and it was the beginning of the end.
The masks she wore were the reason she had sur-
vived a time in her life when she was invisible. At
the beginning of her career they gave the impression professional criticism never stung. So while
her heart thudded erratically, she donned a mask
of Zen-like calm. 'Am I supposed to be intimi-
dated by that?'

He smiled dangerously in reply. 'Keep challenging me and this is going to get real interesting, real quick.'

'Seriously, you're hilarious. I never knew that about you.' Raising a hand, she patted him in the centre of his broad chest. 'Now be a good boy and treat yourself to an early night. Can't have those good looks fading, now, can we?' She flattened her palm and pushed him back to make enough room to open the door. 'What would we use to fool members of the opposite sex into thinking we're a catch if we had to rely on our personality?'

'You tell me.'

Moving her hand from his chest, she wrapped her fingers around a muscled upper arm and encouraged him to step through the door with another push. When he was standing in the hall and looking at her with a hint of a smile on his face, she leaned her shoulder against the door frame and angled her chin. Her eyes narrowed. It felt as if he knew something she didn't.

She *hated* when he did that.

'Admit it: you missed this.'

Lifting her gaze upwards, she studied the air and took a deep breath. 'Nope, can't say I did.'

'Without me around there's no one to set you straight when you need it.'

'You say that as if you know me well enough to know what I need.' She shook her head. 'You don't know me, Daniel. You're afraid to get to know me.'

'Really,' he said dryly.

'Yes, really, because if you did you might have to admit you were wrong about me and we both know you don't like to admit you're wrong about anything.' She glanced up and down the hall as if searching for eavesdroppers before lowering her voice. 'Worse still, you might discover you *like* me. And we can't have that, can we?'

Rocking forward, he lowered his voice to the same level. 'I don't think there's any danger of that.'

Jo searched his too-blue eyes, suddenly questioning if he even remembered how the war between them began. Looking back, she realized she didn't; what was it that made him so much more difficult to get along with than every other member of his family? Everyone got to a point where they started to try and make sense of their life. She was at peace with a lot of the things she couldn't change. But since Daniel was the only person she'd ever been immature around in her entire life, she couldn't help but wonder why. Apparently he wasn't the only one in need of a good night's rest.

She rolled her eyes at the momentary weakness. 'Whatever you tell yourself to help you sleep at night.'

'I sleep just fine,' he said tightly. 'You don't need to worry about me.'

'I wasn't—'

'Just do us both a favour and stay out of my business. If you don't, I might start poking my nose into yours.'

'I have nothing to hide,' she lied. 'Do you?'

'Don't push me, babe.'

She managed to stop the words *or what?* leaving her lips, but it wasn't solely the need to strive for maturity. There was something else going on; she could *feel* it. It was more than the chill in his gaze, more than the rigid set of his shoulders or the unmistakable edge of warning in his deep voice. What *was* it?

As if he could read the question in her eyes, Daniel frowned and turned his profile to her. A muscle tensed on his jaw, suggesting he was grinding his teeth together. But even if she had the right to ask what was wrong, before she had the chance, he turned away. When she ended up staring at his door again, she blinked and shook her head.

Well, Day One had been great.

She couldn't *wait* for Day Two.

CHAPTER TWO

'Is it just me or does coffee taste better when they make those little love hearts in the foam? It's funny the things that can make a difference in how we feel.'

JORJA DAWSON had breasts. Considering he was a man and she was a woman, part of Daniel's brain had to have always known that. Fortunately, in the past, they had never been pressed against his chest in a way that made them difficult to ignore.

It was the kind of intel he could have done without.

Judging by the way the tips of those breasts were beaded against the material of her tight-fitting top before she hid them beneath folded arms, the spark of sexual awareness had been mutual. She should just be thankful he had an honourable streak. If she ever found out he'd been as aware of her as she was of him, she would have a brand-new weapon at her disposal. One that, were she foolish enough to use it, would leave him no choice but to launch a counterattack with heavy artillery until she offered her unconditional surrender.

In terms of fallout, it would be similar to pulling the pin on a grenade he couldn't toss to a safe distance.

Number two on his list: *sister's best friend.*

Since every guy on the planet who didn't have long-term plans knew to avoid that minefield, it wouldn't matter if she wore nothing but lacy underwear to go with the shoes he would have been happy for her to wear to bed. She could have pole-danced for him and he would still resist the urge to kiss her.

'Whatever you tell yourself to help you sleep at night.'

When the echoed words led directly to the memory of the unspoken questions in her eyes, he pushed his body harder in the last block of a five mile run. She'd hit a nerve but there was no way she could know he wasn't sleeping. Or that he was sick of waking up bathed in a cold sweat, his throat raw from yelling. It had to stop before he did something stupid in work again or was forced to look for another apartment. He would damn well *make* it stop.

But distracting himself from the problem with thoughts of Jorja Dawson's breasts wasn't the way to go about it.

Slowing his pace to a walk, he shouldered his way into a busy coffee shop and pushed back the hood on his sweatshirt. After placing his order, he looked around while he waited for it to arrive, his gaze discovering a woman sitting alone by the windows. It was exactly what he needed: *another woman.*

Questioning if he was forming a fetish, he started his assessment with her shoes—a pair of simple black patent heels with open toes—before he moved up the legs crossed elegantly beneath the table to a fitted skirt that hugged her like a second skin. *Nice.* Continuing upwards, he was rewarded with a glimpse of curved breast between the lapels of a crisp white blouse as she turned in her seat. Then his gaze took in the smooth twist of dark hair at the nape of her neck in the kind of up-do that begged to be unpinned so she could shake her hair loose. She was even wearing a pair of small, rectangular-framed reading glasses to complete the fantasy.

But when she turned again, he shook his head. Used to be a time he was better at sensing the presence of the enemy.

She looked up at him when he stopped for a paper napkin at the condiment station beside her. 'Are you kidding me?'

'I can't buy a cup of coffee now?'

'You can buy it somewhere else.'

'This is the closest coffee shop.'

'You can have the one two blocks down. This one is mine.' She returned her attention to her computer screen. 'It's my work space every Monday, Wednesday and Friday morning.'

'I must have missed the notice on the door,' Daniel said as he pulled out the chair facing her and sat down. He smirked when she scowled at him. 'Good morning.'

After an attempt to continue what she was doing while he looked through the window at the steady build of people headed to their offices, she sighed. 'You're going to be here every Monday, Wednesday and Friday, aren't you?'

'Not a morning person, I take it.'

'This is your plan?' She arched a brow when he looked at her. 'You're going to be there every time I turn around until you wear me down and I move? Wow…that's…'

'Effective?'

'I was going to say adolescent. I can't tell you how reassuring it is to know the city is in the hands of such a mature example of the New York Police Department.'

When her fingers began to move across the keyboard again, Daniel realized he didn't have the faintest idea what she did for a living. He wondered why. Hadn't needed to know was the simple answer. Though it did kind of beg the question of why it was he needed to know *now*.

Know your enemy and know yourself and you could fight a hundred battles, as the saying went. With that in mind he took a short breath. 'So what is it you do anyway?'

She didn't look up from the screen. 'It's the first time you've been tempted to ask that question?'

'I don't have a newspaper to pass the time.'

'They're on a stand by the door.'

'It's an internet thing, isn't it?'

Long lashes lifted behind her glasses. 'Meaning?'

'You're one of those people who reports their every move every five minutes so the universe can know how much time they spend doing laundry.'

'Yes, that's the only thing people use the internet for these days.' She reached for her coffee. 'It's because working online isn't a physical job, right? Anyone who isn't lifting heavy objects or doing something with their hands instantly earns a low ranking on your Neanderthal scale of the survival of the fittest.'

'You might want to slow down on the caffeine intake. I think you're close to the legal limit already.'

Setting the cup down, she breathed deep and went back to work. 'I write a blog.'

'You can earn a living doing that?'

'Among other things,' she replied.

'What's it about?'

'Don't you have somewhere you need to be?'

'Nope.'

'Fine, then. I can play the "get to know me better" game until you get bored and leave. It shouldn't take long with your attention span.' Lifting her coffee again, she leaned back in her chair and looked him straight in the eye. 'I work for a fashion magazine and as part of my job I write a daily blog on the latest trends and the kind of things twenty-something women might find interesting.'

'You're as deep as a shallow puddle, aren't you?'

'Not everything is about the meaning of life. Sometimes it's more about living it. For some people that means finding joy in the little things.'

'Like spending money on the kind of clothes that will put them in debt?'

'Like wearing things that make them feel good.' She shrugged a narrow shoulder. 'I assume it's how someone like you feels when they wear their uniform of choice.'

'I don't wear a uniform as a fashion statement.'

'You're saying you don't feel good when you wear it?'

'It's a matter of pride in what I do.'

'And doesn't that make you feel good about yourself?'

She was smart, but *that* he'd known. Trouble was she wasn't entirely right. 'It's not as simple as that.'

When her head tilted at an obviously curious angle, he lounged back in his chair. Since she'd given him the opening with the topic of conversation, he openly checked her out. 'I take it the librarian look is in vogue now.'

'It's better than the mugger ensemble you're wearing.'

Lowering his chin, he ran a large palm over the faded U.S.M.C. lettering on his chest. 'I've had this since basic training. It has sentimental value.'

'Wouldn't that suggest you have a heart?'

'Bit difficult to walk around without one.'

'As difficult as it is to survive without sleep?'

Daniel stared at her without blinking.

'Thin walls...' she said in a soft tone that smacked too much of sympathy for his liking before she shrugged. 'Try falling asleep without the television on, you might get more benefit from the traditional eight hours—especially if you're watching something with that much yelling in it. What was it—horror flick of the week?'

'You're worried about me again? That's sweet.' Feeling sick to his stomach at how close he'd been to humiliation, he got to his feet. 'Now I know you spend your nights with a glass pressed to the wall I'll try and find something on the nature channel with whale song in it.' When his trip to the door was halted by the brush of cool fingers against his hand, he looked down at her. 'What?'

Dropping her arm, she avoided his gaze and shook her head. 'Forget it.'

'You got something to say, spit it out.' He

checked his watch. 'I have an appointment with my boss in an hour.'

The statement lifted her chin again. 'Because of what happened yesterday?'

'Hardly the first time I've had my ass hauled across the coals for breaking the rules.'

'You saved a man's life.' She shrugged her shoulders and looked away. 'I'm sure that counts for something.'

She was reassuring him?

'Not that you don't deserve it for doing something so asinine,' she added. 'You could have placed other members of your team in danger.'

That was more like it. It was also pretty much exactly what he expected to have yelled at him in an hour. 'We all do what we gotta do when the situation calls for it.' He lowered his voice. 'You should know that better than most.'

She looked up at him from the corner of her eye. 'And there you go thinking you know me again.'

'Did it ever occur to you that you don't make it easy for people to do that?'

'People who want to make an effort.'

'And how many tests do they have to pass before you talk to them like they have an IQ higher than a rock?'

'Stupid is as stupid does,' she replied with a smile.

'I take it back. If you're quoting *Forrest Gump* at me you obviously need more caffeine.' He placed an apologetic look on his face. 'I'd get you some before I leave but I'm not allowed to buy coffee here.'

'You're the most irritating person I've ever met.'

'See you later, babe.'

'Not if I see you first.'

'Still rusty.' He shook his head. 'Keep practising.'

'How's the challenge coming along?'

'Hmm?' Jo blinked at her erstwhile roomie, a second night of interrupted sleep catching up with her.

He must have moved his bed after the conversation in the coffee shop. The yelling had been further away but, like the first time, when it came it was torture. She doubted anyone could hear a human being in that much pain and not feel the effect of it emotionally.

'The challenge the magazine gave you?' Jess prompted. 'The one where you wear outfits from the centre pages to discover if different images change how people see you? I'm assuming that's why you look like a French onion seller today. Not that the beret doesn't work for you.'

Yes, she liked the beret. It was the kind of thing she'd have chosen herself, especially when it had a little touch of France to it. But since she wasn't supposed to wear anything the magazine hadn't chosen for her...

Lowering her chin, she idly rearranged the crumbs on her plate with the prongs of her fork. Wasn't as if he would tell her what had caused the nightmare if she asked him, was it? That part of not pushing the subject she got. Where it began to get weird started with the fact she hadn't felt the need to talk it through with his sister. His family cared about him. If he was struggling with something that happened when he was overseas they would want to help in any way possible. Not that he would make it easy. Trouble was she couldn't forget how the colour drained from his face when he'd thought she knew.

It felt as if the man she had known and disliked so much hadn't come home and someone new had taken his place. Someone she could empathize with and wanted to get to know better.

It was just plain *weird*.

'Earth to Jo...'

'It's going fine,' she replied as she speared another piece of cake with her fork and popped it into her mouth. 'Mmm, this one...'

When she risked a brief glance across the table at the only person who knew when she was hiding something, Jo was relieved to find amusement sparkling in Liv's eyes.

'You said that about the last two.'

Jo angled her head. 'Remind me again why we're doing this with you instead of Blake?'

'Because he's more interested in the honeymoon than the cake we have at our reception.'

Fair enough. She reached for a second sample of chocolate cake. 'I lied, it's still this one.'

'You know chocolate is a substitute for sex,' Jess commented. 'It's an endorphins thing.'

'It's more than that,' Jo replied. 'You never have to worry if chocolate will call...it never stands you up...and it doesn't mind keeping you company during a rom-com on a Friday night.' She sighed contentedly as she reached for another sample. 'Chocolate is *better* than sex.'

Jess snorted. 'The hell it is.'

'She's young.' Liv nodded sagely. 'She'll learn.'

'If she tried having it occasionally she'd learn a lot quicker.'

'She scares them off.'

Jo waggled her fork in the air. *'Still in the room...'*

It wasn't her fault guys found her intimidating. With the kind of life experience that went beyond her twenty-four years, she was self-sufficient and hard-working with her focus fixed firmly on her career. If there was overtime available, she took it. Holidays people with family commitments didn't want to work, she volunteered. But regardless of her career, she was also very open about the fact she wasn't interested in getting involved, even if she wasn't prepared to explain why. Put everything together it was difficult for guys to envisage her needing them for more than one thing. Though in fairness there were plenty of them who wouldn't see that as a problem.

There was a short debate on the merits of vanilla cream before Jess asked, 'How's our new neighbour?'

'In order to be "our" new neighbour wouldn't you need to be there more than once a week?' Jo smiled sweetly.

'You need reinforcements, you just have to yell.'

'You *like* Daniel.'

'Everyone but you likes Danny.' Jess shrugged. 'He is what he is and doesn't make any excuses for it. There's a lot to be said for that.'

'There's nothing hidden with him,' Liv agreed. 'When we were kids his bluntness got him into trouble, but honestly? We all kind of relied on it.'

Jo was beginning to wonder if anyone knew Daniel as well as they thought they did but she didn't say so out loud. She couldn't. Not without telling them there were *some* things he kept hidden.

'You could try taking the high road,' Jess suggested.

'I get nosebleeds.' Jo frowned.

The chocolate cake was gone and how had they got from the subject of her sex life to Daniel in the space of two minutes anyway? Apart from spending time with the friends it felt as if she hadn't seen much of lately, part of the appeal of the cake tasting had been the opportunity to take a break from him.

'You make a decision on the cake yet?' she asked.

'I'm swaying towards different layers of these three.' Liv pointed her fork at the emptiest plates.

'What's next on the list?'

'Flowers.'

The conversation swayed back towards wedding plans as they left the bakery and made their way past the public library to the nearest subway station. Jess glanced at the steps in front of the large Grecian columns where several men in helmets and bulletproof vests were gathered around one of the stone lions.

'Isn't that Danny?'

Oh, *come on.*

Reluctantly—as Olivia and Jess headed towards him and she lagged a step behind—Jo had to admit the uniform was sexy in a badass/mess-with-me-and-die kind of way. But then she'd always known Daniel had an edge to him. While he could attract women with a smile, he could make grown men cower with just a look. She had seen that look once. When was it? Tyler's thirtieth, which his younger brother deigned to make an appearance at? Yes, she thought that was it. A giant with a brain the size of a pea was foolish enough to manhandle his girlfriend within Daniel's line of sight. All it had taken was that *look* and a quietly spoken *'show the lady some respect'* and he'd backed down with a string of mumbled apologies. When it was over Daniel had simply continued what he was doing as if nothing had happened.

Jo wondered why it had taken seeing him in uniform for her to remember she'd been impressed by that.

'Ladies.' He nodded once in greeting.

Gathering herself together, she stepped forward and gave the answer everyone expected. 'Officer Moron.'

'Really?' he questioned with a deadpan expression. 'When I'm holding a gun?'

'What can I say?' She shrugged. 'Guess I must like living on the edge.'

While she cocked her head in challenge, he shot a brief downward glance at what she was wearing. It lasted less than a heartbeat, was immediately followed by a cursory blink and then his intense gaze locked with hers, leaving her feeling suddenly…exposed. Whether it was because she'd never noticed him looking at her before or because she was more aware of when he did, she didn't know. But neither option sat well with her. Particularly when she suspected the momentary sense of vulnerability she'd experienced stemmed from the sensation he knew she was remembering things she'd chosen to forget.

Jess chuckled at the interaction. 'Hey, Danny.'

He turned on the charm with the flick of an invisible switch. 'Hey, gorgeous.'

Jo inwardly rolled her eyes at her friend's reaction to his infamous smile before allowing her gaze to roam over the crowd. If she focused on something else, with any luck, she could try and pretend he wasn't there. All she needed was something to take her mind off—

Her stomach dropped to the soles of her strappy heels. 'I've got to go.'

'I thought we were going to look at flowers?'

Looking into Liv's eyes, she used the tone that translated into a hidden message. 'I'll call you later.'

'Okay.'

She didn't look at Daniel as she left, but Jo could sense his gaze on her as she merged into the crowd. How it made her feel helped explain the secret she kept from his sister. Only someone with a shadowy secret of their own could understand what it meant to bring it into the cold light of day. Gaze fixed on the figure she could see moving into the park, she shut down emotionally in preparation.

It was the only way she could deal with it.

The dream began a handful of hours before dawn. New faces—a different scenario—but the outcome was always the same. As he jerked back into reality, pulse racing and heart pounding, Daniel wondered why he was surprised at the latest additions. There was nothing the damn thing loved more than new material.

At times he swore he could hear scaly little demon hands being rubbed together with glee.

Grabbing the sweatpants on the end of his rack, he hauled them on and swore when he stubbed his toe on a box on his way to the kitchen. As he reached for a light switch he froze. The second he yanked open the door to the hall she jumped and dropped her keys.

'Damn it, Daniel!' Jo exclaimed.

Leaning a shoulder against the door frame, he folded his arms across his chest. 'Late night or early start?'

It was a question that didn't require an answer; the outfit she had been wearing outside the library said it all. With considerable effort, he dragged his gaze away from the perfect rear poured into tight black trousers that ended halfway down her calves.

'Who made you the hall monitor?' Keys in hand, she stood up tall and turned to face him.

'I'm a light sleeper.'

A brief frown crossed her face before her gaze landed squarely in the centre of his naked chest. The former should have bugged him more than the latter, especially when it was dangerously close to the kind of look that had forced him to move apartments over the years. Instead he was more bothered by the jolt of electricity travelling through his body from the point of impact. The fact she continued staring didn't help. If anything it aided the flow of blood that rushed to his groin in response.

'Isn't it usually the guy who sneaks home after the deed is done?' he asked as if bringing up the subject of her sex life again would distract his misbehaving body. When her gaze lifted sharply, he changed the subject. 'Didn't occur to you that having a cop for a neighbour might involve him greeting you with his service weapon if he hears you creeping around in the dark?'

'The lights are on,' she argued.

'It's the middle of the night.'

'I don't have to answer to you.'

'Do you have any idea how much paperwork I'll have to fill out if I accidentally shoot you?'

She arched a brow. *Accidentally?*

'That's what I'll call it.'

A lump appeared in her cheek as her gaze searched the air. 'That's twice in twenty-four hours you've threatened to shoot me. I wonder if that's enough for a restraining order. Remind me to ask your sister.'

'He tossed you out of his apartment, didn't he?'

'What is it with this sudden obsession with my sex life?' She looked into his eyes. 'If I didn't know any better I might think it's been a while for you.'

Longer than he cared to admit, but it wasn't as if he could share a bed with a woman for long. He could guarantee his complete and undivided attention while he was there; took a great deal of pride in that fact. But when it came to leaving them satisfied, there was just as much emphasis on the word *leaving*. Preferably before he was dumb enough to fall asleep and risk making a fool of himself.

'Worried I might be lonely, babe?'

She scowled. 'Don't call me babe.'

'If the shoe fits…'

'You know by saying that you're saying you think—?'

'You don't have to like someone to think they're hot.'

'I… You…' When her mouth formed words that didn't appear she clamped it shut, took a short breath through her nose and snapped, 'What are you doing?'

Damned if he knew but the fact it had flustered her worked for him. 'Isn't he a little old for you?'

Something unreadable crossed her eyes before she blinked and lifted her chin. 'Who are we talking about?'

'The guy you were with in Bryant Park.'

'What guy?'

Nice try, but Daniel had never been known to give up that easily. 'The one you argued with before you dragged him into the subway station.'

'You were spying on me?'

'You think when I'm dressed like that I'm supposed to ignore what's happening around me?'

She sighed heavily and turned away. 'I don't have the energy for this.'

'It's Wednesday. We'll pick it up in the coffee shop.'

'No, we won't.'

As her door opened he saw her shoulders slump as if she'd been putting considerable effort into disguising how exhausted she was and the proximity to home allowed her to relax. Most folks were the same at the end of a long day but Daniel knew it was more than that. If he hadn't, he would have got it when she glanced over her shoulder.

Long lashes lifted and for a split second what he could see in her eyes made him frown. He recognized it because he'd seen it in the eyes of men in combat and guys who'd been on the job as a cop for too long. Given no other choice he might have admitted he had been avoiding looking for it in his own eyes in the mirror of late.

If a person's eyes were really the windows to the soul, part of hers was close to giving up the fight.

He took a step forward before he realized he was doing it, compelled by the need to say something, but unable to find the words. With the men he had worked with they were never needed. There was a silent understanding, an empathy born from shared experiences. A nod of acknowledgement could say as much as a hundred words.

Cracking jokes or discussing something inane was more welcome. But someone as full of life as Jo shouldn't—

When her door closed with a low click, Daniel made a snap decision. It wasn't as if he had much choice. If she was in trouble and his family knew he hadn't done something, they would make the roasting he got from his captain look like a weekend barbecue. Taking a long breath, he stepped back and closed the door. In order to prepare for battle he was going to need a few more hours of—hopefully uninterrupted—sleep.

Come daylight he was venturing into enemy territory.

CHAPTER THREE

*'We all know a new outfit can lift our spirits.
But how often do we look at the person wearing
one and wonder if it's a hint of something bigger happening inside?'*

'COME on, Jack, pick up.'

Jo rubbed her fingertips across her forehead to
ease the first indications of a massive headache.
Touching the screen to turn the phone off, she set
it down on the table beside her computer. She was
going to have to go over there. It was the only way
she could be certain where he was.

Sighing heavily, she reached for her coffee cup
only to frown at how light it was. If she was going
to get a day's work done in half the time she was
going to need a constant supply of caffeine.

'That his name, is it?'

The sound of a familiar deep voice snapped
her gaze to another coffee cup being held out to-

wards her. She blinked at the large hand holding it. 'Eavesdrop much?'

'Let's call it an occupational hazard.' Daniel rocked his hand a little. 'You want this or not?'

Her gaze lifted, lingering for a moment on his chest when she remembered what it had looked like naked: taut tanned skin over muscle and a six-pack to make a girl drool. Frowning at the memory, she moved further up until she was looking into too-blue eyes and asked, 'Why are you buying me coffee?'

'You looked like you could do with it,' he replied.

'You don't even know how I take it.'

'Since you're a regular, I surmised the guy behind the counter would. Turns out I was right.'

Jo's gaze lowered to the temptation as she weighed up the risk involved with accepting it. Not that he would wait for an invitation to join her, but apart from the fact she wasn't in the mood to get into a verbal sparring match with him—

'Your loss.' He shrugged. Setting it down on the opposite side of the table, he pulled out the empty chair and sat down.

'There are other tables in here, you know.'

Daniel didn't say anything, his steady gaze fixed on hers as he took the lid off his cup.

'We're not picking up where we left off last night, if that's what you're thinking,' she said.

'Technically it was this morning.'

'I've stayed out of your business.'

'Glad to hear it.'

'How about you return the favour and stay out of mine?' She smiled sweetly, determined not to look at the abandoned coffee on the table in front of him.

Daniel brought his cup to his face and took a deep breath. 'Nothing quite like a cup of Joe to kick-start the morning...'

While her eyes narrowed at the innuendo, he lifted his other arm and tapped the lid of the abandoned coffee cup with a long forefinger. 'Sure you don't want this? Seems a shame for it to go to waste...'

'What do you want?'

'Suspicious, aren't we?'

'I've met you.'

'And still not a morning person.' He inclined his head towards the cup. 'Another shot of caffeine might help.'

Jo fought the need to growl. She wanted that

coffee so badly she could taste it on her tongue. Despite her strong-willed determination to stop it happening, her gaze lowered to watch the tip of his forefinger trace an almost absent-minded circle around the edge of the plastic lid. It was one of the most sensual things she had ever seen, adding a new dimension to the temptation, which had nothing to do with caffeine. For a moment her imagination even wondered what the movement would feel like against her skin...

Reaching out, she waggled her fingers. 'Give.'

His hand moved, fingers curling around the cup to draw it back towards him. 'How much trouble are you in?'

Her gaze snapped up again. 'What?'

'Answer the question.'

'Why would you even care if I was in trouble?' She arched a brow. 'I'd have thought the idea of my body lying in an alley somewhere would have made your day.'

'Is there a chance that might happen?'

'Not like it would be the first time.'

'That's not funny.'

'No, but I have dozens of jokes from that period of my life if you need them.' Angling her chin, she pulled one at random from the air. 'You know the best part about dating a homeless chick? You can drop her off wherever you want.'

Daniel didn't laugh. 'Do you owe him money?'

'Owe who money?'

'Jack.'

'No.'

'Then what's going on?'

A short burst of laughter left her lips. 'I'm supposed to confide in you because you bought me a cup of coffee?'

'If you're in some kind of trouble, tell me now and—'

'You'll help?' The words came out more sharply than she intended and, when they did, she felt a need to soften them by adding, 'You can't, and even if you could you'd be the last person I'd go to for help.'

Great, now he was never going to leave it alone. She might as well have dangled a scented cloth under the nose of a bloodhound.

'I'm aware of that,' he said flatly.

'Then why are you doing this?'

When she thought about it, she realized it was simply what he did. All she was to him was another citizen of the city of New York. One he probably felt pressured to help because of her connection to his family. She shook her head. She didn't need this, least of all from him.

'Tell me what's going on.'

The tone of his deep voice inflicted more damage than anything he'd said or done in five and a half years to get to her and she hated him for it. Mostly because the rough rumble was accompanied by a softening of the blue in his eyes, which made it feel as if he understood. As always when there was the slightest danger someone might see through one of her masks, Jo fought fire with fire. 'I'll tell you what's going on when you tell me why it is you can't sleep.'

To his credit he disguised his reaction better than he had before. But the second the softer hue of his eyes became an ice-cold blue, Jo regretted what she'd said. She shouldn't have thrown it in his face. Not to get at him. It was *low*.

'What makes you think I'm not sleeping?'

Jo wavered on an indecisive tightrope between familiar ground and freefalling into the unknown. 'You were awake in the middle of the night. And you still look tired.'

'I work shifts. And it's not always easy to adjust,' he replied without missing a beat. Stretching a long arm across the table, he set the coffee beside her computer. *'Your turn.'*

It would have been if he'd told her the truth.

'You've been a cop for, what, eight years now?'

'More or less.' He nodded. 'And can have your every move reported back to me if I have to. Your point?'

'How long does it take to adjust?'

'I was overseas seven months. I've been back one.'

'What happened when you were over there?'

'We got shot at.' Lifting his cup to his mouth, he took a drink without breaking eye contact. 'Avoid the subject all you want, but we both know if I want to find out what you're hiding I can do it without your co-operation. I'll start with Liv.'

It was an empty threat. Jo reached for the coffee he had given her. 'Your sister won't tell you anything.'

'Meaning she knows what it is.'

'Meaning she wouldn't betray a confidence.'

A corner of his mouth tugged upwards. 'You know my family. They'll organize an intervention if they think something is wrong. If you've never been on the receiving end of one I can tell you they're a barrel of laughs. Nothing beats a little quality family time when it's five against one. And I did say I'd *start* with Liv...'

'What makes you think you're not the only one who doesn't know?' she asked.

'If I am you've just made it easier for me.'

The message blood was thicker than water was clear. But she wasn't so far removed they wouldn't rally to her aid if she needed help. Jo had known that for years. They were all cut from a cloth threaded with loyalty, honour, integrity and at least a dozen other positive attributes she'd had absolutely no experience of in a family until she met the Brannigans. To Jo, they were everything a family should be. It was part of the reason she'd never understood why Daniel didn't appreciate them more. But the comment he made about family interventions explained a lot. It was an insight into why he was fighting his demons alone.

She lifted the coffee cup to her lips. 'When you speak to them you should mention the problems you're having adjusting to shift patterns. Your brothers might be able to offer some words of advice.'

'Maybe you should just tell me what's going on before this starts to get ugly,' he smirked in reply.

'We could do this all day.'

'Next round's on you. I take mine black.'

She sighed. 'You're not going to back down, are you?'

'Not my thing.'

'Which brings us back to why you need to know. Correct me if I'm wrong, but I don't think you've answered that yet.'

When he didn't reply, she set her coffee down and went back to work, answering some of the comments on her blog while he reached across to the next table and lifted an abandoned newspaper. They sat in silence for a while until Jo could feel a tingle along the back of her neck. Without lifting her chin, she looked up from beneath her fringe to discover him studying her intently. 'What?'

'Were the glasses a fashion accessory?'

She focused on the screen again. 'I get headaches if I work at the computer for too long.'

'So where are they?'

'I left them in the apartment.'

'Other things on your mind…' he surmised.

'I can make the print bigger on the screen if you're so concerned about my eyesight.'

There was another moment of silence, then 'Just out of curiosity, what look is it you're aiming for today?'

'It's called Gothic chic.'

At least that was what the magazine had called it. Of all the outfits she had worn during the challenge it was the most outlandish. But since she'd awoken with a need to face the world with a little more bravado and it was the kind of outfit that required confidence to carry it off...

'Might want to remember vampires aren't supposed to walk in direct sunlight before you step outside,' he said.

'Are you going to tell me to avoid holy water, garlic and crosses too?'

He nodded. 'And teenage cheerleaders with wooden stakes...'

Turning in her chair, Jo stretched her legs and pouted. 'You don't like the boots?' she asked as she looked at him. 'They're my favourite part.'

Daniel leaned to the side to examine them, a small frown appearing between his brows. 'You can walk in those things?'

'Women don't wear boots like these for comfort.'

Bending forward, she reached down and ran her hands over the shining leather, tucking her thumbs under the edge at her thigh and tugging as she lifted her foot off the ground. Her hair fell over her shoulder as she turned her head and smiled the kind of small, meaningful smile she'd never aimed at him before. 'Didn't we talk about how people wear things because of the way they make them feel?'

The glint of danger in his eyes was obviously intended to make her stop what she was doing before she was any deeper in trouble. *Foolish man.* He really didn't know her at all.

Daniel gritted his teeth together as she repeated the motion with her hands on her other leg and tossed her hair over her shoulder as she sat up. When she smiled across the room, his gaze followed her line of vision to the barista who was smiling back at her.

The one who had known how she took her coffee.

The second his gaze shifted, Daniel glared at him. But the guy who immediately went scurrying back to his coffee beans wasn't the source of his annoyance. Neither was the fact his plan to purposefully avoid looking at her feet as he approached the table had backfired on him, though, with hindsight, forewarned might have been forearmed. What got to him was how well her diversionary tactic had worked.

There wasn't a male cell in his body that hadn't reacted to those boots and the strip of bare skin below another sinful short skirt. He had spent every moment since he'd sat down with her consciously stopping himself from looking at the straining buttons on her black blouse and once again she'd got him with footwear. But if she thought it would distract him from his target for long, she was mistaken.

He was a Marine, for crying out loud; the phrase 'courage under fire' was as good as tattooed on his ass.

Watching with hooded eyes, he saw her slide her computer to one side before resting her elbow on the table. Setting her chin in her palm, she leaned forward, feigned innocence with a flutter of long lashes and asked, 'Something wrong?'

'You done?' he questioned dryly.

'Done with what?' Amusement danced in her eyes. 'You might need to elaborate.'

If he didn't know what she was doing, he might have been tempted to play along. But if he did, Daniel knew what would happen. He would play to win.

'Tell me what's going on.'

When she rolled her eyes, he set his forearms

on the table and leaned closer, his gaze locked on hers while he waited. Up close she did have pretty spectacular eyes. A little large for her face maybe, but they were so deep a brown it was difficult to tell where the irises began.

He'd never noticed that before.

After studying him for a long moment, she lowered her voice. 'What if I told you it was private?'

'I'd tell you I won't share it with anyone else,' he replied in the same low tone.

'Why should I believe you?'

'A man is nothing without his word.'

'Tell me why you need to know.'

He wondered when she thought he'd handed over control of the negotiation. Dragging his gaze from mesmerizing eyes, he considered what to tell her. She was right; they could do this all day. Until one of them bent a little nothing would ever change. Of course knowing that meant he had to ask himself if he *wanted* their relationship to change. But since it felt as if it already was…

'I recognized what I saw in your eyes before you closed the door this morning.' He looked into them again as he spoke. 'I've seen it before.'

'What did you see?' she asked in a whisper, forcing him to lean closer to hear her.

'Resignation.'

She stared at him and then blinked as if trying to bring him into focus. 'If you knew me as well as you like to think you do, you'd know...'

'I'd know?' he prompted as she frowned.

'Why I don't want to talk about it.' Dropping her palm from her chin, she leaned back and swiped a strand of hair behind her ear. 'People keep secrets for a reason.'

When she reached for her computer, Daniel felt the lost opportunity as keenly as he sensed she wasn't just talking about herself. But if she knew the reason he wasn't sleeping, why hadn't she pushed the advantage? Lifting his coffee cup, he looked out of the window and questioned what he would have done if their places had been switched. The exact same thing was the honest answer. It was what he was doing already. He knew there was something wrong and was giving her an opportunity to tell him. In turn, she was refusing to open up.

Number four on his list: *nothing in common.*

So much for that one...

'You want another coffee?' she asked.

He looked at her cup from the corner of his eye. 'What did you do, inhale it?'

'Figured if you were planning on digging in, I may as well top up on supplies.'

Since sitting still for any amount of time inevitably led to reminders of his sleep deprivation, Daniel shook his head. 'Think I'll head down to the station and look through mugshots for Jack before my shift starts.'

Jo sighed heavily as he stood up. 'Dig all you want. I'm telling you now there's only one way you'll find out and that avenue isn't and never will be open to you.'

'And there you go challenging me again...'

Taking a step forward, he set his coffee cup hand on the table by her computer and the other on the back of her chair. As her chin lifted he leaned down, smiling the same kind of small, meaningful smile she'd aimed at him when she'd pulled her little stunt with the boots.

'When I want something, nothing gets in my way,' he told her in a deliberately low, intimate tone. 'Make it difficult for me, I'll want it more and work twice as hard to get it. So feel free to keep doing what you're doing, but don't say you weren't warned.'

When her eyes widened he leaned back, lifted his hands and turned away. She could interpret his words any way she liked. If she came to the conclusion he was talking about more than the secret she was keeping, he wasn't certain she'd be wrong.

Gothic chic was either going to be the death of her or get her arrested. For starters, her feet were killing her, but if she'd known she would end up walking the length and breadth of her old neighbourhood looking for Jack she would have changed. When it came to getting arrested, she might be grateful. Even if the charge was related to standing still for too long on a street corner as she tried to get her bearings, she could take comfort from the knowledge she was safe in the back of a squad car. When she looked over her shoulder and thought she could see someone moving in the shadows, her pace quickened.

If Daniel saw where she was, she could imagine the lecture she'd get on personal safety. There hadn't been a single set of flashing lights she hadn't looked at twice or an echoing siren that hadn't turned her head. Every time it happened she would find herself thinking of him and what he'd said before he left the coffee shop.

He couldn't possibly have meant what she

thought he meant. But what was worse was her reaction. Instead of being outraged or angry or laughing in his face, she had been turned on, *big time*. Her breath had caught, her pulse had skipped, and her breasts had ached. She'd even had to press her thighs together. No man had ever had such an immediate erotic effect on her.

That it was *him*?

A shiver ran down her spine, forcing her to look over her shoulder again. Ridiculously she wished he were there, but in her defence she was starting to get seriously creeped out. The presence of a six-foot-two police officer could have made her feel better, even if they argued every step of the way.

Taking a breath, she shook off her paranoia. She could take care of herself. Harsh truth was, until Liv, the only person she had ever been able to depend on was herself.

Tugging the edges of her long black coat together in an attempt to hide what she was wearing, she stopped and looked up at the neon sign before opening the door. If Jack wasn't in there she swore he was on his own this time.

'Well, *hello, gorgeous*! You want to come over here and—'

Jo glared at the man who stepped in front of her. 'I have pepper spray and I'm not afraid to use it.'

She didn't, but he didn't know that.

'Mikey, leave the lady alone,' a voice called from behind the long wooden bar. 'She's *way* out of your league.'

She smiled when she got there. 'Hey, Ben.'

'Hey, Jo,' he beamed in reply. 'How's my best girl?'

'She's good. He here?'

Ben nodded. 'Back room.'

'He run up a tab?'

'Made a deal with you, didn't we?'

'Thanks, Ben.'

Jo made her way through the crowd, regretting how much time it had taken to get through her work so she could begin the search. If she'd got away earlier, not only would it not be dark outside, it wouldn't have got to the point where she had to attempt to carry Jack home. She sighed heavily.

Ahead of her was the inevitable debate about whether or not it was time to leave. She knew exactly what he would say, the excuses he would make, how many random strangers she would have to be polite to while she gritted her teeth. It was a scenario she'd experienced countless times.

No matter how far she managed to get from her past, she could always rely on Jack to remind her of her roots.

The thought of Daniel being able to do the same thing...

She rolled her eyes. *Enough with the thinking about him, already!* It was getting to the point where it felt as if he were with her wherever she went.

Daniel leaned back against the wall and frowned. Any guilt he might have felt about tailing her had disappeared within five minutes of arriving at her destination.

What the hell had she got herself into?

Judging by the number of times she did a double take at passing police vehicles or lifted her chin when she heard a siren, it wasn't anything good. He waited to see if she spent the same two minutes in the eighth bar as she had in the other seven. When she hadn't reappeared after twenty minutes he was contemplating crossing the street. Then the doors opened.

The man staggered back a step as she helped him get his arm into the sleeve of his coat. He had obviously been in the bar for a lot longer than she had. Placing his arm across her shoulders, she wrapped one of hers around his waist before steering him along the sidewalk.

What was she doing with a guy like that? Apart from the fact he was twice her age, she shouldn't be with someone she had to go searching for in bars. Daniel was disproportionately disappointed in her considering their relationship. He might have made several digs about her sex life, but a woman who looked as she did, who was as smart as she was and could turn a guy on the way she'd—

Grinding his teeth together hard enough to crack the enamel, he thought about finding the nearest subway station. Why should he care what she was doing when she plainly didn't? But before he could leave the man staggered sideways, slammed Jo into a wall, and something inside Daniel snapped.

Reaching a hand beneath the neck of his sweater to pull out the badge hanging on a chain around his neck, he checked for traffic and jogged across the street. Once he'd caught up to them, he set a firm hand on the man's shoulder and pushed him back a couple of steps. 'NYPD—you, over there.' He pointed a finger at Jo. 'And *you* stay right where you are.'

Her eyes widened in disbelief as he turned towards her. 'You're following me now?'

'Cop, remember? What did you think I was gonna do?'

'You're *unbelievable*!'

'And you're damn lucky you had a bodyguard for the last couple of hours considering where you are. What the hell did you think you were doing coming out here alone? Do you have any idea the number of shots-fired reports we get from this neighbourhood?' When her companion staggered forward, Daniel glared at him from the corner of his eye. 'I wouldn't if I were you, buddy. I'll tell you when you can move.'

The man lowered his chin, his words slurred. 'You can't talk to my—'

'Shut up, Jack,' Jo continued, frowning at Daniel. '*How dare you*—?'

'Oh, I dare,' he replied. 'What's more, you're going to tell me exactly what's going on and you can do it here or you can do it at the nearest precinct. *Your call.*'

'You can't *arrest me.*'

'Wanna bet?'

'I haven't *done* anything!'

Daniel nodded. 'Okay, then, I'll arrest him. Seems to me he could do with a night in a cell to sober up.'

When he turned, a hand gripped his arm.

'Don't.' The dark pools of her eyes sparkled as she let go of his arm, gathered control and lowered her voice. 'I just need to get him home.'

Going to the nearest precinct felt like the better option to Daniel, but something stopped him. She was still angry—he could feel it radiating from her in waves—but he had been in enough situations to know when there was more to the story. It made him wish for better light so he could search for a clue. If he'd had a flashlight he would have aimed it at her eyes.

Taking a long, measured breath, he gave *good old Jack* the once-over while making his decision. 'How far?'

'Four blocks.'

'And you were planning on carrying him there?'

'Daniel—'

'You lead the way, I'll bring him, and when we get there we're having a long talk.'

'You *think*?'

Crossing his jaw as he watched her turn and

walk away, Daniel reached out a hand and grabbed hold of a sleeve before the man next to him fell over. 'Throw up on me and I'm still arresting you.'

The journey took twice as long as it would if all three of them had been able to walk in a straight line. Most of which an impatient Daniel spent shutting the guy down every time he tried to start a conversation. Once they got there Jo ushered the older man into the bathroom of a sparsely furnished one-bed apartment. Daniel paced the small living room while he waited. Then something caught his eye.

Stopping in front of a set of bookshelves, he reached out and picked up a framed certificate that had been presented to Jorja Elizabeth Dawson for perfect attendance in the sixth grade. Lifting his chin, he then discovered a photograph propped against a pile of books further in. It was a younger Jack standing in front of what looked like a Ferris wheel, his arms around a skinny kid with long, dark pigtails and a huge grin that revealed two missing front teeth.

Daniel realized his mistake in an instant and the second he did felt like the biggest jackass on the face of the earth. Glancing at the hall from the corner of his eye he found Jo watching him in silence.

'He's your father,' he said with certainty.

'Yes,' she replied.

'You should have told me.'

'If I'd wanted you to know, I would.'

After placing the certificate back on the shelf, he turned towards her and shoved his hands into the pockets of his jeans. 'How long has he been drinking?'

'It would be quicker to tell you when he wasn't.' She shrugged a shoulder and damped her lips with the tip of her tongue as she avoided his gaze. 'It's worse one month than the other eleven. This just happens to be that one month.'

When she looked at him, Daniel experienced a sensation he'd never felt before. Inwardly squirming didn't quite cover it. Not when it felt as if his internal organs were trying to crawl away and find a place to hide.

He took a deep breath. 'Jo—'

The door behind her opened and Jack appeared, taking an uneven path from wall to wall until he stopped and swayed on his feet. As Jo turned towards him Daniel stepped forward and freed his hands.

'I owe you an apology for the misunderstanding.' He held out an arm and shook her father's hand. 'Daniel Brannigan. I'm a friend of your daughter.'

There was a soft derisive snort from his right. 'Bit of an exaggeration, don't you think?'

'I was worried about her.'

'Since when?'

Considering he deserved whatever she tossed at him, Daniel sucked it up and looked her straight in the eye as he added, 'I thought she was in some kind of trouble.'

'Not my Jo,' Jack slurred. 'She's a good girl.' He dropped his chin and squinted. 'You're a cop?'

'Yes.' Swearing inwardly, Daniel reached for his badge to tuck it away. 'Emergency Services Unit.'

'People need help they call 911.' Jack grinned. 'Cops need help they call the ESU.'

'That's us.' Daniel nodded.

'You want a drink?'

'Good luck finding one,' Jo interjected. 'I cleaned you out last night.'

Daniel shook his head. 'No, thank you. I'm just gonna see your daughter home safely if that's okay with you.'

'That won't be necessary,' she said tightly.

He looked into her eyes again, his tone firm. 'It's the least I can do.'

'Okay.' She smiled sweetly. 'We can have that talk you wanted on the way back. While I get Jack settled, how about you have a *good long think* about the things you want to say to me?' Scrunching her nose in mocking delight, she placed an arm around her father's waist. 'Come on, Jack, let's go.'

As they left Daniel dropped his head back, stared at the ceiling and took a deep breath.

It was going to be the longest subway ride of his life.

CHAPTER FOUR

'Don't you love it when you find something you forgot you bought in the sales? It's true what people say: look closely and you might be surprised what you find.'

'YOU know what this reminds me of?'

Daniel's gaze shifted to tangle with hers from across the compartment. 'We're talking now, are we?'

'No. I'm talking. You don't get to speak yet.'

As the train slowed he glanced out of the window behind her. Jo had a sneaking suspicion he was counting down stations in the same way an imprisoned man might mark off the days of his sentence on a wall. But if he thought she'd forgive him because he'd had the sense to keep his mouth shut since they left Jack's place…

'It reminds me of the number of times I've heard my best friend complain about her brothers running background checks on every guy they ever saw her with.' She angled her head in thought. 'I used to think it was funny, now not so much...'

'We were looking out for her,' he said flatly.

'Why can I hear you?'

When he breathed deep and exhaled in a way that suggested he was running out of patience, she folded her arms. 'Beats me why you didn't put one of those tracking anklets on her.'

'If you mean a tether, we considered it.'

It was exactly the kind of opening he should have known not to give her. 'What gives you the right to interfere in other people's lives?'

'It's called concern.'

'It's called harassment.'

'I'm not going to apologize for following you.'

Her brows lifted. *'Excuse me?'*

'While you were giving me the silent treatment, I had time to think it over.' Stretching long legs, he spread his feet a little wider and shrugged. 'Considering where you ended up I'm not sorry I followed you. From now on, if you have to go there at night, I'll be going with you.'

Oh, no, he wouldn't. 'I'm not your sister.'

'I'm more than aware of that,' he replied tightly.

'You can't tell me what to do.'

'No. But I can tell you how it is.' Briefly glancing at the other passenger in the compartment, he brought his legs back towards him. Leaning forward, he rested his elbows on his knees and lowered his voice. 'Something happens to you I won't have it on my conscience. It's crowded enough already.'

When she frowned he leaned back, his profile turned to her and the muscle working in his jaw-line. Jo wanted to stay mad at him, still hadn't forgiven him and refused point-blank to be told what she could and couldn't do. But at the same time—much as she'd prefer if it didn't—the insight softened her a little, especially when telling her had obviously cost him something. It was his way of making amends, wasn't it?

Drumming her fingers on her arm, she tried to decide if she felt like being reasonable. On the one hand, she'd been conscious of the fact she was alone at night in an area where she was likely to get mugged, or worse. On the other, she'd grown up in that neighbourhood, could take care of herself and wouldn't have been so creeped out if she hadn't been *followed*.

It wasn't that she didn't appreciate the concern for her safety—as unexpected as it was coming from *him*—or that he'd apologized to Jack and shown respect to a man many people would at best have pitied. It was just, if she was honest, it stung that he knew.

Everyone had things they weren't comfortable with other people knowing. As he'd been when he told her something he had to know would leave her more curious than before...

Darn it, she really didn't want to be reasonable. But he wasn't *forgiven*.

As the train rocked along the tracks she thought about the last time she had to deal with someone who'd learnt about Jack. Difference was with Liv she had been in control what she chose to divulge. Liv hadn't pushed. Liv would never have followed her. But even after six years and with a traumatic experience to bond them together, Jo knew she held things back. It was what she'd done for the vast majority of her life. She didn't think she would ever change.

As he looked out of the window behind her Daniel stood up. 'We change here.'

Jo grimaced when she got to her feet. Determined not to reveal she was suffering in the name of fashion, she grabbed hold of one of the vertical metal bars while they waited for the train to stop and the doors to slide open. Walking with an enviable ease to the other side of the platform, Daniel looked over his shoulder and stilled.

'What's wrong?'

'Nothing,' she answered through gritted teeth.

Turning, he studied her feet while she focused on the bench in the middle of the platform. 'Would kill you to ask for help, wouldn't it?'

'They're blisters, not broken legs.'

As she sat down he turned to check the tunnel for signs of an oncoming train before pushing his hands into the pockets of his jeans. Since he took a good long look at her boots when he turned around, Jo leaned back on the bench and allowed her coat to fall open. Resting her palms on the plastic beams, she crossed her legs. When his gaze shifted sharply to the extra inches of thigh the move revealed, she stifled a satisfied smile. Knowing she could get to him had always helped, even if the rash impulse to discover just how much she affected him in *that way* probably wasn't the best idea she'd ever had.

With a single blink, his gaze snapped to attention and locked with hers. She jerked her brows in reply.

It earned an almost imperceptible shake of his

head. 'I'd heard women don't wear boots like that for comfort.'

Goosebumps erupted on her skin when she heard his voice. Deeper, rougher, it conjured up the kind of thoughts her self-preservation was forced to stamp with 'CENSORED' before her imagination provided the images to go with them.

'These boots definitely weren't made for walking,' she mused as she rocked her crossed leg.

'Begs the question of why you didn't think to change.'

Jo angled her chin. 'You have a real problem with what I'm wearing, don't you? Don't tell me you prefer your women in crinolines. Carrying a parasol maybe? Someone who will drop her handkerchief and swoon as you pass by...who'd be *eternally grateful* when you come to her rescue...'

'You really gonna go there?'

It would seem so. She shrugged a shoulder. 'It's half your problem with me. Neanderthal man meets modern-day, independent woman and he doesn't know what to do with her.'

The smile was slow, deliciously dangerous and steeped in heady sensuality. 'You have a lot to learn about a man like me, babe. When you're ready to find out, let me know.'

She would have called him on the 'babe' thing again if the invitation hadn't felt like six-foot-two of blue-eyed Death by Chocolate. But there was no way she was letting what he'd said slide. 'Is that supposed to scare me?'

'What makes you think that's what I was aiming for?'

'You think I can't take you on and win, Danny?'

He smiled again. 'I'm Danny now, am I?'

An answering smile formed on her lips before she realized it was happening. When it came, his smile grew.

Thought he had the upper hand, did he? Well, in that case, she might have to give in to the impulse to find out how much of an effect she had on him. Rationalizing it as the need to know what she had to work with, she lifted her chin, stretched her arms out to her sides and arched her back. Purposefully pushing her breasts forward in a way she knew would strain the buttons on her blouse to the breaking point, she parted her lips and took a deep breath. To top it off, she shook her hair off her shoulders, caught her lower lip between her teeth and let it slowly slide free. When she was done she looked at him.

A burning gaze travelled the length of her body

and back up. It lingered on her breasts for a moment, making them swell against the decadent lace of the bra she'd forgotten she had until she went digging in a drawer for the kind of underwear befitting her outfit.

When his gaze found hers, he nodded. 'You do like living on the edge.'

There it was again: that deeper, rougher voice…

It was beyond tempting to ask what he planned to do about it. But before she could weigh up the risk the opportunity was lost to the sound of an oncoming train.

Stepping over to the bench, he held out a large palm and jerked his chin. 'Up.'

Jo stared at his hand as brakes squealed and a rush of air whispered strands of hair against her cheeks. But she couldn't back down, not after her show of sexual bravado. Sliding her palm across his, she felt the same jolt of heat travel up her arm she had experienced the first time he touched her. By the time long fingers closed around hers and he tugged her to her feet, it was spreading over her entire body. Drawing a long breath, she avoided his gaze by looking over a wide shoulder at the train. As it stopped she took a tentative step forward and grimaced when her ankle turned.

The grip on her hand tightened. 'You got it?'

The question raised a small smile. 'You tell me.'

Threading his fingers through hers, he stepped forward to push the release button on the train doors. Holding them open with his arm to allow her to step inside, he leaned closer to inform her, 'I know what you're doing.'

'Do you?' she questioned over her shoulder as the doors slid shut behind them.

'Mmm-hmm,' he replied with a firm nod, his too-blue eyes darkening as she turned and looked up at him.

When the train jerked into motion, she rocked forward, a low gasp hauled through her lips when her breasts made contact with his chest. If it felt as good as it did with layers of clothing between them the thought of skin-to-skin was enough to form a moan in the base of her throat. She tried to take a step back, but a long arm wrapped around her waist, holding her in place as he lowered his head and spoke into the hair above her ear.

'How close do you want to get to that edge?'

Jo's heart kicked against the wall of her chest, her blood transformed into liquid fire.

Turning his hand against hers, he made enough room to rub his thumb against her palm, the long fingers of his other hand splayed possessively over her hip. 'If you're curious what's on the other side, I can take you there.'

His low, rough voice made the words *take you* sound like a promise of ecstasy. A distant whispered *yes* echoed inside her and made her slide her lower body across his. When Daniel tensed in response and the fingers on her hip pressed tighter, a surge of feminine empowerment washed over Jo.

Turning her head, she lifted her chin and spoke in an equally low tone into his ear. 'This would be working a lot better if you *stopped talking.*'

'Someone who makes a living with words should know what they can do.' The hand at her hip slid dangerously close to the curve of her rear. 'Only takes a few and our minds fill in the rest.'

Jo took a breath of clean, masculine scent and resisted the urge to rub her cheek against his jaw. 'It takes the *right* words.' She smiled languidly. 'And I think you'll find I have the advantage there...'

'Lay a few on me and we'll see.'

What they were doing should have felt weird but didn't. If anything it felt like an adult version of the 'fun' she needed to draw her back from the past. She glanced at what she could see of his face. Instead of fighting her attraction to him the way she knew she should, she decided to enjoy the ride. Just for a little while. She'd never had a male playmate before but it was an exhilarating experience. Especially with a Marine-turned-cop she could go toe-to-toe with on equal terms…

The movement of the train rocked their bodies while his thumb traced circles in her palm. His head moved a fraction, the millimetres of space between her cheek and his jawline tingled with static. 'Chickening out on me, babe?'

As if. Lowering her voice to an even more intimate level, Jo carefully enunciated each word. 'Anticipation…longing…*desire*…' Lifting her hand, she set her palm on his upper arm, curling her fingers around the dark material of his jacket and the tight muscles underneath. 'Heighten…intensify…quicken…' She sighed breathily as her hand moved up his arm and across a shoulder to the rigid column of his neck. 'Tighten, strain, grasp, reach—' She gasped, held her breath for a second and exhaled on a blissful sigh. 'Release.'

'*Jorja.*'

The growled warning made her lean back so she could see his face. What she'd done might have ended up doing more for *her* than she'd planned, but it was obvious it had done just as much for him. His eyes were as dark as storm-filled skies. Waves of the kind of tension that could only be eased with physical satisfaction rolled off his large body, seeped into hers, and made her ache for the satisfaction to be mutual. When his gaze lowered to her mouth, it elicited an unintentional swipe of her tongue in preparation.

She wondered what kissing him would feel like…

Okay, that was enough. She really needed to snap out of it. She couldn't hand him a victory like that when he would never let her forget it. Daniel equalled arch nemesis. Any *other* guy who had the same effect on her equalled candidate for the kind of sex she obviously needed more than she'd realized.

Dropping her chin, she looked up at him from beneath heavy lashes. 'I have another word for you…'

'Trouble?'

'*Disappointment*. I'd learn to live with it if I were you.' Adding a sweet smile, she dropped her hand from his neck to his chest and pushed as she looked over a shoulder. 'Look at that, it's our stop. Doesn't time fly when you're having fun?'

Stepping onto the platform ahead of him, Jo held her arm out to her side to regain her balance before she let go of his hand. Without warning he yanked her back towards him. As she stumbled a large hand wrapped around the back of her neck and the world as she'd known it came swiftly to an end.

Firm lips crushed hers in a bruising kiss that rocked her back on her heels. She squeaked in surprise, blinked wide eyes and grasped hold of his shoulder to stay upright. But when he canted his head, she closed her eyes. As it always had in every other aspect of their relationship, her competitive streak kicked in. He couldn't light up her body like a roman candle on the fourth of July without repercussions.

Absorbing the intensity of the kiss, she bundled it into a fist in her chest and tossed it back at him. Her lips parted. His tongue pushed inside, duelling with hers. It was angry and messy and uncoordinated and without a doubt the hottest kiss she'd ever experienced and Jo *hated him* for that. She didn't want to spend the rest of her life comparing every kiss to one and have the rest fall short. Not when it was obviously meant to punish her for what she'd done to him on the train.

He just couldn't back down and let her win one, could he?

He didn't know *how*.

When the kiss ended as suddenly as it began, Jo's eyes snapped open, the sound of ragged breathing making her realize the train had left. She stared up at him. To her surprise he didn't look at all victorious. If anything he looked as angry as she felt. Without saying anything, he released her, turned and headed straight for the exit. She gritted her teeth and followed him to give him a piece of her mind, frowning with frustration when her feet wouldn't allow her to match his long stride. As he reached the turnstiles Daniel glanced over his shoulder. When he turned and marched right back towards her, Jo froze. What was he—?

She was swept off her feet before she had time to figure out what he intended. 'Put me down!'

'We go at your pace we'll be lucky to get back before Thanksgiving,' he said tightly.

'I can still *walk*.'

'The expression on your face that suggests it's over broken glass says otherwise. Stop squirming.'

Lifting her higher, he turned sideways and

pushed his leg against the turnstile. His gaze was fixed firmly ahead, his jaw set with determination; she knew there wasn't a hope in hell he would put her down any time soon. *Fine, then,* he wanted to carry her for two blocks, he could go right ahead. She hoped he strained something while doing it. Sighing heavily, she placed an arm around his neck. When they hit the sidewalk and a passer-by smiled, she pointed at her feet.

'Blisters,' she explained before the woman got the idea what she was seeing was anywhere in the region of romantic.

'Ah,' the woman said in reply.

Having started, Jo found the prospect of talking to random strangers infinitely preferable to talking to *him.*

'Lovely evening.'

'Yes, it is.'

She swung her legs a little and tried to ignore the fact a large hand was wrapped around her knee. 'Enjoying the city?'

A couple wearing the obligatory 'I heart New York' T-shirts lifted their gazes from the map they were poring over. 'Yes, thank you. It is wonderful.'

'Wait. Go back,' she demanded before craning her neck to look at the tourists. 'Are you lost?'

Daniel sighed impatiently before turning, remaining silent while the couple held the map out. Jo offered directions and tips for places to visit. Smiling brightly, she then enquired where they were from and said she hoped they enjoyed the rest of their trip. She even got to try out some conversational—if a little on the rusty side— French. They were a lovely couple.

'You going to do this the whole way back?' Daniel asked as he started walking again.

Jo ignored him and looked around. 'Hi, how are you?'

'I'm good, how are you?'

'I have blisters.' She pouted.

When he finally shouldered his way into the foyer of their apartment building, he headed for the stairs.

'If we'd taken the elevator you wouldn't have to carry me any more,' she pointed out after the second flight.

'We rescued two people stuck in an elevator yesterday. It occurred to me at the time if I ever got stuck in that ancient contraption the guys would never let me hear the end of it.'

'Two people stuck in an elevator.' She pondered. 'I wonder what they did to pass the time…'

'Two *men* stuck in an elevator.'

'I wonder what they did to pass the time…'

He glanced at her. 'Forgiven me for following you yet?'

It didn't escape Jo's attention he hadn't mentioned any forgiveness for kissing her. But either way her answer was the same. 'No.'

Eight flights later and—to her great irritation—without Daniel so much as breaking a sweat, they were at her door.

'Key,' he ordered.

'You can put me down now.'

'Key.'

Tugging on the strap across her breasts, she removed her arm from around his neck to unzip the small bag at the end of it and dig for her keychain. Lifting it in front of his face, she jangled it for effect. 'Happy now?'

'I will be when you put it in the door.'

'And how exactly am I supposed to do that from way up here?' When he simply leaned forward, she muttered under her breath, 'Planning on tucking me into bed too?'

'That an invitation?'

'I can't believe you just said that out loud.' Swiping her hair behind her ear, she focused on getting the key into the lock and turning it.

Daniel carried her inside, waited for her to hit the light and then kicked the door shut. Unceremoniously dumping her on the cushions of the sofa, he sat down on the chest she used as a coffee table and raised a palm. 'Give me your foot.'

Jo wriggled up the cushions, swiping her hair out of her eyes. 'You're kidding me, right?'

'I'm not leaving till I see how much damage you've done. Give me your foot.'

'Sure you're not trying to sneak a feel of the boots? You know you can get therapy for that, right?'

'It's amazing to me you've lived this long without someone strangling you.' He waggled long fingers. 'The sooner you give me your foot, the sooner you can get rid of me.'

'Well, when you put it *that* way…' Raising her foot, she set it on his knee, her pulse thrumming while she waited for the opening she needed to slap him.

Daniel ran his palms along her boot. When he got to the top Jo pressed her lips together at his expression. He didn't deserve a smile for the hesitation.

'Problem?' she asked.

'No.'

'The zip is at the back.'

'I know.'

'Do you also know in order to take it off you're going to have to touch me?' Seemed to Jo it hadn't been an issue before he dumped her on the sofa.

His gaze lifted and locked with hers as a heated palm set against the back of her thigh drew a gasp through her lips.

'It doesn't go any higher than that,' she warned.

A low rasp sounded as he opened the zipper. Slipping long fingers under the edge, he pushed the leather down her leg and lifted her foot with his other hand. As the boot descended his hand smoothed over her skin, distracting her from the sharp sting at her ankle with an excruciatingly gentle caress.

Despite how mad she was at him for kissing her, there wasn't an inch of her body that didn't ache for that touch. But since it was Daniel, she still couldn't wrap her head around it. Her heart hammered erratically. Had he changed or had she? Heat seeped into her skin and travelled back up her leg. When had it happened? *How* had it happened? Her pulse sang with intense pleasure. Who cared when it felt so good?

Setting the boot aside, he lowered his gaze and ran his palm up her calf. Jo swallowed in an attempt to dampen her dry mouth, caught her lower lip between her teeth to stop another moan from escaping. She really should put a stop to what he was doing. In a little minute, she vowed she would.

Leaning to the side as one hand smoothed over the top of her foot, he used the long fingers curled around the back of her calf to lift her leg so he could look at her ankle. 'Is the other one as bad as this one?'

That deep, rough voice again…

Jo silently cleared her throat. 'Probably.'

Oh, good, now *her voice* sounded different.

'Let me see,' he demanded.

One. More. Minute.

Setting her foot on the floor, she raised her other leg and held her breath while he repeated each slow move. With a second opportunity to take everything in, the way his hands touched the leather felt reverent, the way they smoothed over her skin more decadent. She should have been prepared for the effect it had on her knowing what he could do with a kiss, but she wasn't. Jo doubted anything could have prepared her for what felt like tenderness, especially from a man like him. If he added tenderness to a kiss, would it still be as hot? She should *not* want to know the answer to that question as badly as she did.

'You have a first-aid kit?' he asked.

'Mmm-hmm.'

His gaze lifted, a smile forming in too-blue eyes when she didn't say anything else. 'Want to tell me where it is?'

'Bathroom.'

'I'll find it. You stay here.'

Once he stood and walked away, Jo hauled a breath into her aching chest and exhaled it with puffed cheeks. Time seemed to be slipping from her grasp along with her sanity. That minute was bound to be up. Her eyes widened when she remembered what the first-aid kit was sitting beside in her bathroom cabinet. He'd better not think *that* was an invitation.

But when he reappeared, Daniel simply set the first-aid kit on the chest, sat down and reached for her foot again.

'I can do that,' Jo said when she found her voice.

Selecting what he needed, he ripped open a small white package and curled a hand under her calf. 'As appreciative as I am of your footwear, you should consider flats from time to time. This might sting.'

'Ouch!'

A corner of his mouth lifted as he reached for a Band-Aid. 'They're blisters, not broken legs.'

'And now he's funny again.' She frowned as he swapped one foot for another. 'Could you get a move on?'

'Almost done.'

She gritted her teeth. After he smoothed a second Band-Aid in place, she snatched her foot back.

''Night, Daniel,' she hinted heavily.

He pushed upright, but instead of standing straight he leaned over her, his gaze locked with hers. Jo's eyes widened when he laid his hands on the cushions at either side of her hips. What was he doing? Her stupid, errant tongue damped her lips in preparation as his face angled over hers.

He couldn't seriously... She shouldn't want... She lifted her chin an unconscious inch. But instead of kissing her, Daniel stilled and a devastatingly sexy smile formed on his mouth.

''Night, babe,' he said in *that* voice.

Jo blinked as he crossed the room and she heard the door close. Now he knew what he did to her, he would use it every opportunity he got. Reaching to her side for a throw cushion, she pressed it tight to her face and screamed in frustration.

CHAPTER FIVE

'Much as I adore summer, I love the rich colours of the fall. Breathe deep right now and even in the city you can sense the approach of something spectacular.'

SHE started it. Hardly the most mature response, but, since he had spent every waking hour replaying the hottest kiss of his life over and over in his mind, Daniel didn't care.

Even the fact she was who she was didn't make a difference any more, particularly when he took into consideration how he'd reacted to the box that had greeted him directly at eye level as he opened her bathroom cabinet. It wasn't that he didn't think it was sensible to have them there. It wasn't as if she'd been unfaithful to him or he'd been a saint since the day they met either. But for a split second it had been hard to resist the urge to bring the box back with him, toss it in her lap and demand she told him who she'd used them *with*.

As it was, he had slammed the cabinet shut and swore there was only one man she would be using them with in the not-too-distant future. She might have unwittingly caught his interest with a pair of red stilettos, but she knew exactly what she'd been doing on the train. Just as he knew exactly what would happen if she discovered he was attracted to her and used it against him.

Unfortunately, when he'd rolled out the heavy artillery, he'd discovered he was dealing with guerilla warfare. She'd hit him hard and fast, disappeared behind the woman who'd bugged him with very little effort, then hit him again when he attempted a temporary ceasefire by doing something *nice*.

Those boots had a lot to answer for.

He liked to think he'd launched an effective counterattack before he'd left her apartment. She was angry he had kissed her. Most likely wasn't any happier she'd kissed him back. But she had made it obvious she was open to it happening again. The way Daniel saw it, considering there hadn't been a whole heap of finesse involved in their first kiss, his next step was to right that wrong.

Taking a stealth approach, he entered the coffee

shop by the door furthest from her table. While waiting for his order he did a little reconnaissance. She wouldn't catch him out the same way twice. Starting with her hair—since it was as far as he could get from the danger zones—he discovered a sleek ponytail. His gaze moved lower to discover a white dress and what looked like a low scooped neckline—needed to be ready for that one, then. Lower still and he frowned as he wondered if there was a worldwide shortage of skirt material. When he remembered how soft her skin was at the back of her thighs he tore his gaze away. He wasn't convinced he could handle what was on her feet. Not when his body was primed for a lot more than a kiss.

'Figured it was too good to last,' she muttered as he set a coffee cup beside her computer and sat down.

'Miss me?'

'How about you disappear for more than thirty-two hours and we'll see if it helps any? A decade might do it.'

Easing the lid off his cup, Daniel stared at her and waited to see how long it would take for her to crack under pressure. To her credit she lasted longer than he expected. In the end it took a yawn she covered with the back of her hand to break the silence.

'Did you go see Jack again last night?' he asked. Since she didn't reply, he took it to mean 'yes'. 'I thought we'd agreed you wouldn't go there alone.'

'Don't remember agreeing to that.'

He reached out a hand. 'Give me your cell phone.'

The demand lifted her gaze. 'Am I grounded, too?'

'No,' he replied. 'But you're about five seconds away from a curfew. *Phone.*'

'What do you want it for?'

'I'm going to put my number in it. The next time you have to go there at night, you'll call me.'

'No, I won't.'

Daniel rested his elbow on the table while he took a drink of coffee.

'You can hold your hand there till you get cramp. I'm not giving you my cell phone.' She focused on her screen again. 'I don't need a bodyguard and you work shifts. Not like you can drop everything and come running to my aid if you're working at night, is it?'

'If I'm on duty, Tyler will go with you.'

'Again, don't need a bodyguard—but if I did I have Tyler's number on speed-dial.'

Daniel frowned when his mind decided to make a connection between his brother and the box in her bathroom cabinet. 'I'm not kidding around here, Jo. Give me the damn cell phone.'

The sharp tone lifted her gaze again. Whatever it was she discovered when she searched his eyes softened her voice. 'I can take care of myself.'

'Humour me,' he replied with more control.

'Not something I'm usually prone to do...'

'Make an exception this time.' He used a beckoning motion with his fingers. 'If it helps tell yourself just because the number is there doesn't mean you'll use it. We can argue that one later.'

Angling her chin, she pouted and thought it over. 'I don't suppose you'll consider going away once the number is there?'

'Not till I drink my coffee.'

She brightened. 'Can you drink it faster?'

'Any particular reason you're uncomfortable with me being here?' he enquired.

Avoiding his gaze, she shrugged. 'No more than usual.'

Daniel smiled. Now he knew what to look for, she sucked at lying. 'If you don't give me your cell phone I can make this cup last all day.' He purposefully lowered his voice. 'There's a lot to be said for taking things slowly…'

Frowning, she lifted a pile of papers, produced her cell phone and reached out to drop it in his hand. Wasn't prepared to risk touching him, was she?

His smile grew. 'See now, was that so difficult?'

'Pushing your luck,' she said as she looked at her screen and lifted her fingers to the keyboard.

Daniel entered his number, sending a text to his phone so he had hers. When he was done, he held his hand up, her phone dead centre in his palm.

She glanced at it. 'You can put it on the table.'

'You want it, come get it.'

'With lines like that I can see how you're the equivalent of catnip to the ladies…'

With a small sigh, she reached out. When her nails scraped against his skin, every muscle in his body jerked in response. His fingers closed around hers. Full lips parted, her breasts rising on a sharp inward breath as she looked into his eyes.

'Tell me you'll call me,' he said.

'You said we'd argue about that later.'

'That was a couple of minutes ago.' When she tugged on her hand he tightened his hold. 'Say it.'

'Daniel—'

'Why did I follow you, Jo?'

She arched a brow. 'You know if you keep reminding me what you did it's not going to help me forgive you any quicker.'

'Why do you think I did it?'

'You told me why.'

'That I wouldn't have it on my conscience if anything happened to you—still true—but I told you that *after* I saw where you were.' Relaxing his hold a little, he brushed his thumb over the soft skin on the back of her hand as he lowered his arm to the table. 'Now ask yourself why I followed you in the first place.'

'It's what you do.' Her gaze was drawn to the movement of his thumb.

'Not with everyone. Not enough hours in the day...'

'Not what I meant. You're a cop and a Marine, your whole life is based on a sense of duty towards others. You figured you had to get to the bottom of it because of my relationship with your family.'

Daniel nodded. 'That's what I told myself.'

She slipped her hand free and lifted her chin. 'It's not that I don't appreciate your concern—'

'Concern would be part of it,' he allowed as he

set her cell phone down. 'Same kind of concern you felt for my safety when I unhooked my harness on the bridge that day.'

'That wasn't concern for your safety.' She scowled. 'It was incredulity at your stupidity and anger at your lack of consideration for the people who care about you.'

'You'd have been fine if I fell.'

'Wasn't the fall that would have done the damage, it was hitting the water that would have got you killed.'

Daniel kept pushing. 'You'd have been okay with that?'

'Of course I wouldn't have been okay with it. You *know* what it would have done to your family.'

'But you'd have been fine.'

'I'm not having this conversation any more.' Grabbing her cell phone, she slammed it down on the pile of papers before flicking her ponytail over her shoulder and aiming the scowl at her screen. *'Go away.'*

Daniel took a breath. 'We may have been arguing since the day we met, but we've known each other for almost six years. It's difficult *not* to care about someone who's been there that long.

Something happens, you notice the gap left behind. Might take a decade for you to miss me, but I like to think you'd get round to it if you knew I wasn't coming back.'

Fine-boned fingers stilled on the keyboard as her gaze focused on an invisible point in the air a couple of inches above the screen. During the following silence Daniel tried to figure out if he regretted what he'd said. He probably should, if for no other reason than the fact it explained her second appearance in his nightmare.

'Why are you telling me this?'

The question was asked in so low a voice he almost missed it in the ambient noise of the coffee shop. While he reached for the lid of his cup, he considered the answer.

Getting them to the point where they both accepted the inevitable conclusion of their volatile attraction was one explanation. It was certainly the one at the forefront of his mind. But the fact he wasn't firing on all six cylinders might have had something to do with it. If he hadn't been driven by the need to pick up where they'd left off, he could have tried grabbing some sleep before he went looking for her.

Too late now...

It was bound to happen at some point. Focus was the first thing to go, swiftly followed by hand-to-eye coordination; the latter of which probably explained the reason he was having so much damn difficulty putting the lid back on his cup.

He frowned at it in annoyance.

Resisting the need to yawn when she yawned had been more than a natural reflex. It was a reminder his body could only run for so long on adrenalin alone. His work provided regular top-ups. As did spending time with Jo with the electricity of their attraction constantly crackling in the air between them. But strip those things away and Daniel was bone-tired, off his game and a shadow of his former self.

'You asked if I ever got tired of this...' It was as close as he could get to the heart of the problem without giving too much away. 'Maybe you were right.' When he managed to slot the lid into place, he stood up. 'On that note, since I covered half of someone's shift this morning and I'm back in at four, I better get some sleep.'

He was at the door when she stopped him.

'Danny?' She turned in her seat to look at him.

'Yes?'

'If I need help, I'll call.' The concession was

followed by a lift of her brows to indicate it was his turn.

'You won't go there alone at night.'

She shook her head. 'I can't make that promise.'

'You'll change before you go and you'll be *careful*.'

'I'm always careful.'

'Flat shoes, loose clothes.' He waved a hand up and down. 'The kind that cover you from head to toe…'

The smile in her eyes wavered on her lips. 'Should I put a bag over my head?'

'A ski-mask would probably help you blend in more easily in that neighbourhood.' When she rolled her eyes, he fought a smile of his own. 'First sign of trouble, you call.' He nodded his head at her cell phone. 'My number's under H.'

'I've said I…' She blinked. 'Why is it under H?'

Cutting the smile loose, he reached for the door. She was checking her phone as he passed the window, what looked like a burst of laughter leaving her lips before she shook her head.

He might have ended up saying more than he'd intended, but he was definitely gaining ground.

* * *

Of course she would notice if he were gone for ever. Did he really think she was so detached from her fellow human beings?

She would probably have got mad at him if he hadn't caught her off guard. It was his voice to begin with—the words laced with sincerity. But what got to her was the slight tremor to his hand when he put the lid back on his cup. While he frowned at it, she studied him: the lines of tension at the corner of his eye, a slight hint of grey beneath his tan. Added to the secret she kept for him, they lent a deeper meaning to the question she'd asked the night he moved in. Jo would dare anyone not to stop and think about how they felt after that. Even if they weren't convinced they wanted to know the answer.

Closer to the top of the well of memories she'd chosen to forget, she remembered how he looked the last time she saw him before he went overseas. It was one of the rare occasions he'd made an appearance at Sunday lunch and the last time he sat in his place opposite her at the table. She remembered how laid-back he'd been while an underlying note of tension in the room had said everything about his family's concern for his safety.

Had she taken the time then to think about

what it would be like if he hadn't come home? If the chair opposite hers had remained empty for as long as his father's before the family moved around the table? She would like to think she had. But she couldn't remember worrying beyond keeping an eye on the news reports, wondering where he was if anything happened to a Marine. It was the same thing anyone would have done if they knew someone in a war zone. But when it came down to it she'd assumed how she would feel if something happened to him would be attached to his family. If they were hurting, she'd hurt for them. Grieving, she would feel grief for their loss. Part of the trouble was she'd never been able to remove his family from the equation. She still didn't.

But for the first time she thought about how she'd feel if it was just Danny and Jo and then Danny wasn't there any more...

She *would* miss him. Who would she argue with the way she argued with him? But it couldn't be anything more. Jo knew all about the gap a person could leave behind and what it did to people who loved them. She could never allow herself to care about someone so much she disappeared into that hole.

Not after she'd watched it happen to someone else.

Having spent a good portion of her time in the
coffee shop staring into space, she returned to
the apartment. An entire day at home during the
week was a rare luxury when more often than
not she was running all over Manhattan by mid-
afternoon. So after checking in with the office
to discuss images for her assignment and catch
up on the gossip, she settled down with some
freelance work. The first time she thought she'd
heard something, her gaze lifted from the computer. Shaking her head when she found nothing
but the usual city soundtrack running in the background, she went back to work.

There it was again.

Pushing back her chair, she walked to her bedroom door where it was muffled, but louder.
When it stopped, she held her breath and waited,
heart twisting the second it started again. It was
no less torturous during daylight hours than it was
at night. Did he *ever* sleep? She glanced across
the room at the large clock on the kitchen wall. It
was almost three. Hadn't he said he had to be in
work at four? The dilemma made her waver on
her feet. He would *hate* that she knew.

A text to her 'Hot Neighbour' wouldn't be any better than turning up at his door. Either way there had to be a reason she knew he was there and might be late for his shift. She could say she hadn't heard his door close but then he might think she was listening for his movements. Up until, well, a few hours ago, if she was honest, she'd rather have poked red-hot needles in her eyes than allow him to think that.

The second hand on the clock sounded a 'Don't. Let. Him. Be. Late.' with each tick in the silence broken by an agonized cry from beyond the wall.

Okay, that was it. She was going over there.

When the door yanked open, the sight of a naked muscled chest made her breath catch—forcing her gaze sharply upwards. What she found didn't have any less of an effect, albeit in a different, more worrisome way. His eyes were red, his jaw was tense and he frowned as he blinked her into focus.

It did something to her heart she had to ignore.

Lifting an arm, he rested a large hand on the edge of the door by his head. 'What?'

'You said you had to go to work at four.' She held out a mug. 'You're going to be late.'

A brief glance at his wristwatch was swiftly followed by a low expletive before he lifted his gaze and his eyes narrowed. 'How did you know I was still here?'

'I didn't,' she lied with a shrug. 'Thought I'd check…'

His frown darkened. 'You shouldn't do that when you're not any good at it.'

When she didn't say anything, his gaze searched the hall. Suddenly slicing through the air, it slammed into her, driving the air from her lungs.

'Since the first night?' he asked grimly.

Jo nodded.

A shadow crossed his eyes, revealing something she never expected to see. Coming back at him had always been easy when he was cocky and in control; tossing jibes the equivalent of bouncing pebbles off an armoured tank. He knew who he was, what he was capable of, was calm under pressure and unwavering when it came to what he wanted. She supposed there had always been something she found sexy about that, even when they argued.

But the tiny crack in his control, the mere hint of a vulnerability that made it feel as if he desperately needed something he hadn't found? It echoed deep inside Jo where she kept her own vulnerability hidden. Unlikely as it would have once been, she wanted to be the one to give him that missing something. She just wished it didn't feel as if the one thing he needed was the one thing she could never give him.

'Thanks for the coffee.' He reached out and took the mug from her hand. 'And the wake-up call.'

Jo took a step forward when he stepped back. 'Danny—'

'Don't.' A large hand nodded once in a 'calm down' move she suspected wasn't solely for her benefit. He took a deep breath, crossed his jaw, looked anywhere but at her, and then used his forefinger to emphasize each word. 'Just...*don't*...'

When the door swung shut in her face, Jo stared at it for a long time without moving. Whatever headway they had made in the coffee shop disappeared like early morning mist. Crossing the hall had been a mistake. Why couldn't she have left it alone?

The answer was simple: She *did* care.

Probably more than she should.

'Damn it!' Daniel threw his gloves at the truck.

'We can't save them all,' his partner said flatly.

'Two inches, Jim.' He demonstrated the distance with a gap between his thumb and forefinger. 'All

I needed was *two inches* and I could have put pressure on the artery.'

'And once we'd freed his leg he could have gone into shock and died anyway. You know that. Let it go.'

Except he couldn't let it go, could he? Not so far away there were scaly little hands rubbing together in glee. Didn't take a genius to work out what he would see in his nightmare the next time he closed his eyes, did it? Daniel's gaze sliced through flashes of red and blue neon reflected on rain-soaked surfaces to the collapsed wall several ESU squads had been working on. The man who had died had gone out for a carton of milk, walked past an abandoned building at the wrong time and that was that. Game over.

When they had arrived at the scene Daniel had volunteered to crawl inside a narrow space deemed unsafe for a paramedic. He'd been there for three hours as he talked to the guy to try and keep him conscious while they dug him out. Mike Krakowski, forty-three, wife, two kids, somewhat ironically—possibly because the universe had a sick sense of humour—a construction worker. Mike had lost consciousness a half-hour ago and when his pulse stopped beating there hadn't been a damn thing Daniel could do about it.

His partner slapped his shoulder. 'Walk it off, brother.'

Pacing around the emergency vehicles, he tried to roll the tension out of his shoulders and neck. He *hated* that Jo knew. The thought she knew because she had heard him yelling made it worse. There was only one thing he wanted to see in her eyes and sympathy wasn't it. So much for gaining ground...

He wondered how the residents' committee felt about subletting on a short-term lease. Moving from hotel to hotel the way he had after he landed stateside wasn't an option Daniel favoured, having tried it. Wasn't as if he could spend a night on someone's sofa either and he sure as hell couldn't go home. A handful of hours in the room he shared with Tyler growing up and keeping his distance from his family would have been a complete waste of effort.

Not for the first time, he missed the respite of being overseas. Turned out the scaly-handed little sucker hadn't liked the background noise of bullets firing and exploding shells. Frightened of losing its plaything, Daniel assumed, since a lack of sleep could have led to a fatal error a lot faster out there. So while many of the men he shared sleeping quarters with would toss and turn on their racks, he'd slept like a baby. He'd been paying for it with interest ever since.

Heading back to the truck to help pack away the equipment, he decided avoiding Jo for a few days was the only option open to him. Much as beating a retreat went against every instinct the Marine in him possessed, he didn't have a choice.

The next time he faced her, if there was so much as a *hint* of sympathy in her eyes…

Remind him of how much less a man he felt compared to the way he used to be and he'd be honour-bound to prove her wrong. Strong as she was, he doubted she was ready for the full force of that, especially when it had been held inside him for so long. The thought of what was involved got his juices flowing and reminded him how primed he was for more than a kiss, but she was still *Jo*. He wouldn't do that to her. The very fact he reacted the way he did to her knowledge was dangerous enough.

Let her get any closer…

Bending down, he picked up his gloves and tucked them in his back pocket. *Game over.*

CHAPTER SIX

'There's nothing quite like rearranging a closet to make a girl feel she's in control. The smallest of moves can have a domino effect on our lives.'

WHAT did he think he was going to do—assume a new identity and move to another state? It was something he might want to consider, because by Monday—when he hadn't shown up in the coffee shop—Jo was good and mad at him.

It felt as if her body were tuned in to him; didn't matter what time of night it was or how quiet he was on his way into the apartment. Once her subconscious assumed he was restless, she got restless. Before she knew it, she was blinking into the darkness, waiting. When the yelling came, as it inevitably would, for Jo it felt worse than before.

Each night he was shredding a jagged little slither off her heart and his answer to the fact she'd kept her mouth shut to protect his secret was to *avoid her*?

She was going to kick his ass.

Halfway up the second flight of stairs in their apartment block, she heard a familiar deep rumble. Picking up the pace, she arrived—a little breathless and ready to spit nails—at the top of the sixth flight. Rounding the corner she discovered he was talking to the head of the residents' committee.

Heart thudding erratically and unable to blame it *entirely* on the stairs, she gave him the once over. As usual he was in the prerequisite jeans, presently matched with a dark round-necked sweatshirt and a charcoal sports jacket. She had seen him in similar clothes a hundred times, so what was it that suddenly made him more of a feast for the eyes than before? No one had the right to look that good when they hadn't slept in as long as he hadn't so her singing pulse could just *shut up*.

She glanced at the bag in his hand. 'Are those cookies?'

'Freshly baked…' Daniel smiled his infamous smile at their neighbour who behaved liked a giddy schoolgirl in response.

'Danny confessed to a sweet tooth,' she explained. 'Have to look after our boys in uniform when they're away from home, don't we?'

'Yes.' Jo nodded. 'It's a long way to Staten Island.'

Daniel leaned forward and turned on the charm. 'Still too far away from home baking, right, Agatha?'

She patted his arm. 'Let me know when you run out.'

'You're too good to me.'

'Yes, she is.' Reaching out to ruffle woolly white ears, Jo crooned, 'Isn't she, Gershwin?'

When her hand dropped Daniel replaced it with his.

'Bye, little guy. Look after your mom.' As their neighbour left, he tilted closer to her and lowered his voice. 'Did I mention this is the second batch she's baked for me?'

Jo didn't say anything as they waved goodbye but as soon as the door down the hall closed, she swung on him. Aiming a brief glance over a wide shoulder, she grabbed a fistful of dark sweater and backed him into the elevator.

'*Stay,*' she ordered before turning to close the cage door.

Just once was it so much to ask the stupid thing to close without having an argument first?

'Need a hand with that?' a deep voice enquired.

'Don't make me hurt you.' It took several angry

attempts to achieve her goal before she pressed the button and turned on him again.

Leaning against the back of the cage, he reached into the bag before tilting it towards her. 'Fresh-baked cookie?'

'I hope you choke on them.' She folded her arms over her breasts. 'How long are you planning on avoiding me?'

'That's what I'm doing, is it?' Taking a bite of toffee pecan, he leaned his head back and frowned as he studied the creaking mechanism above their heads.

Jo was too mad at him to play games. 'You think you're the only one losing sleep since you moved in across the hall? But did I say anything? No. What I did was make sure you weren't late for work. Thanks for that, Jo. No problem, Daniel. That's all it would have taken. We could have gone on pretending I didn't know. Instead you asked, I answered and now you've decided to punish me for not lying when *apparently* I wasn't any good at it to begin with.'

When his gaze locked with hers, a warning sparkled in his too-blue eyes.

She sighed. 'Our apartments wrap round the

building. We share a wall. How long did you think you could hide it?'

Daniel tossed what was left in his hand back into the bag. When his gaze lifted to the appearance of their floor—despite the speed of the elevator—Jo could sense she was running out of time. What would it take to get through to him?

'Why do you think I didn't say anything, Danny?'

It was a question she would prefer not to answer, but even the softening of her voice wasn't enough. His shoulders lifted a very visible inch and the knuckles of the hand holding the bag went white. Ridiculously, it felt as if she was losing him.

As the elevator shuddered to a halt he stepped forward and looked her straight in the eye.

She lifted her chin. 'I'm not moving.'

Setting his hands on either side of her waist, he simply lifted her out of the way and set her down at the back of the elevator. When he did Jo dropped her arms and lost it.

'You can't avoid me *for ever*!'

As if it knew not to mess with him, the cage door moved with one sharp tug. The second he stepped into the hall, he turned and yanked it shut again.

Her eyes widened. 'What are you—?'

Reaching through the cage, he hit the button to send her back to the ground floor.

Forget kicking his ass. She was going to *kill him*.

If he'd been in a better mood the expression on her face as the elevator descended would have made him laugh out loud. Instead he turned and walked away.

He didn't get far before her voice sounded.

'Go ahead and avoid me for the next fifty years. Up until a few days ago you could have gift-wrapped that for me and it would have been the best present I've ever been given!' There was a pause he presumed was to allow her to take a breath. But when she spoke again he could hear something new threaded in her voice. 'I'm not angry you don't want to talk about it. I get that part. Probably better than you think. But they'll be selling ice cream in hell before I try talking to you again.'

Daniel stilled and took a long, calming breath. It wasn't what she said, what got to him was the note in her voice that almost sounded...*hurt*.

Shaking his head, he headed for his apartment. He'd been tossing pointed verbal spears at her for years without leaving a mark but a silent response had hit the target?

How did *that* work?

He'd braced himself for several things when he laid eyes on her again. With hindsight the stand-to-attention greeting from his body should have been higher up the list. But when it came to the things he knew he would struggle with most like sympathy, pity—hell, even being *nice* to him would have done it—there hadn't been one. Instead he got the kind of response he should have known to expect from her. Not only had she called him on what he was doing and set him straight, she kicked him to the kerb for punishing her for something that wasn't her fault. It was the note of hurt in her voice and his answering guilt for causing it that said the most about the change in their evolving relationship.

Stepping out of the hall, he closed the door and found his gaze drawn across the room to the item on the kitchen counter.

By the time she made it to the top of the stairs he was leaning on his door frame, ankles crossed and a hand held out in front of him. Gauntlet casually swinging on his forefinger, he watched from the corner of his eye as she glared at him before pointedly focusing on her destination. When she came to a halt in front of him she pressed her lips together, took a breath and looked at his finger.

'Is that my mug?'

He let it swing a little harder. 'Yes.'

'I hate you.'

'I know.'

Snatching the mug, she fitted her key in the lock, stepped inside her apartment and slammed the door. Daniel stayed where he was and waited.

Four, three, two...

The door swung open again.

'You know what I hate most?' she snapped.

'That you didn't think of the elevator trick first?'

'I *hate* that you can make me this mad.'

He nodded. 'It's a talent.'

'I'm normally pretty Zen about the universe, despite everything it's thrown at me. But you— *you* bug the hell out of me.' She waved a hand at his face with attitude. 'That whole "nothing gets to me" façade you got going on bugs me more than anything. Especially now I know it's a big fat lie.' Her eyes widened when a slow smile began to form on his face. '*Really*, you're doing that *now*? When I've just told you I can see right through you?'

'I doubt that.'

If she could see right through him she would know he was thinking how beautiful she was when she was angry. He'd always thought it was a cliché but with Jo it was true. She flashed fire from her eyes; the full force of a passionate nature he'd only got glimpses of in the past made it difficult not to cross the hall. It didn't matter if she unleashed all of her inner fire on him, erupted in an inferno and left him in a pile of sated ashes. If anything it made him want her more.

'Don't do that,' she warned.

His smile grew. 'What am I doing?'

'You know what you're doing.'

'Thinking about coming over there so we can make up?'

'We don't have that kind of relationship.'

'Didn't use to,' he allowed.

'Just because we made an attempt at trying to be friends doesn't mean—'

'That's what you're calling this?' He raised his brows in disbelief. There was no way she could be that naïve.

'I—'

'You're telling me you haven't thought about it.'

She opened her mouth, closed it and then opened it again. 'What are we talking about?'

'I think you know what we're talking about.'

'You mean sex.' She frowned at his chest. 'With you…'

'I was talking about the kiss in the subway station, but if you want go there…'

'I haven't thought about it,' she lied.

Daniel shook his head. 'We've already established you shouldn't do that when you're not any good at it.'

'You're telling me you *have* thought about it?'

'If you mean sex…with you…'

Her eyes narrowed.

'I'm a guy, of course I've thought about it.'

She lifted her chin. *'And?'*

Daniel shrugged in a way he hoped didn't give away the fact just talking about it was turning him on. 'I think two people who spark off each the way we do could have pretty spectacular sex. You don't?'

'I meant the… Yes… *No…* I mean I don't know much about—'

'Spectacular sex?' The fact he had flustered her again brought a knowing smile to his mouth. 'You should try it. There's a lot to recommend it.'

'Wasn't where I was going.' She frowned.

'No?'

'Would you quit that?'

'What am I doing now?'

'Looking at me like a man looks at a woman.'

'Bit difficult to avoid...' His gaze travelled the length of her body, lingering on her breasts.

'That's second-date territory you're in right now.'

'We've had coffee three times.'

She gasped in outrage. 'Those weren't *dates*.'

Unable to resist any longer, Daniel nudged his door frame and stepped forward. 'When it comes to the kiss in the subway station, I think we can do better.'

'Danny, stop.' Her tone was suddenly more of a plea than a warning. She took a step back. 'You and me? *Huge mistake*.'

Reaching out, he took her hand and brought her back to her door frame. 'Who are you trying to convince?'

Before she could reply, he released her hand and framed her face. The tip of her tongue swiped her lips, moistening them in preparation as her gaze lowered to his mouth. When she looked up, doubt flashed across her eyes. He would have used every lesson he'd learnt from the seduction handbook to remove that uncertainty. But as his head lowered her chin lifted and their mouths met before he was ready.

A jolt of electricity zipped through his body. At first he froze, determined to ignore muscles that jerked in response so he could carry out his plan to demonstrate more finesse. He wanted to savour her, spend hours kissing her.

Starting with her mouth…

Capturing her lower lip first, then the upper, he drew from the experience of a lifetime of kisses that paled in comparison. If he'd known kissing her could feel so good, they'd have been doing it a lot sooner. When a breathy sigh escaped her lips, he breathed it in; the first brush of his tongue against hers met with a low hum of approval at the back of her throat. While she simply stood with her spine against the door frame and allowed him to explore, it was easier to control the pace and the demands of his body. The second her hands flattened on his stomach and she started doing a little exploring of her own, his control was tested as it had never been tested before.

The need to thrust against her was excruciating, but he forced himself to settle for pinning her to the door frame with his body. The desire to palm one of her perfect breasts was agonizing, but he forced himself to settle for a hand on her ribcage. Minutes dissolved into nothing but nipping, licking, and the kind of restless hand exploration that skirted them close to the point of no return. In the end it was the woman who was supposed to be lost in the moment *with him* who broke the kiss to point out a different kind of danger.

'Danny...' she mumbled. 'Elevator...'

Listening for long enough to hear someone fighting with the cage door, he leaned back in. Knowing that door they had at least another couple of minutes.

But Jo ducked out of the way, her voice thickened by the drugging effect of desire. 'We're not the only people who live on this floor.'

'They live at the opposite end of the hall,' he replied in a rough voice, which said just as much about the effect desire was having on him. 'But if it's doing it for you go ahead and think about getting caught...'

'You're *bad*,' she whispered.

'I haven't even got started yet,' he whispered back.

To prove his point he allowed his hand to slide

up her ribcage so the tip of his thumb could brush the underside of her breast. Her kiss-swollen lips immediately parted on an inward, stuttered breath, head turning as she attempted to look down the hall.

'They can't see what I'm doing,' he reassured her.

She looked into his eyes again. 'Didn't I say where you're headed right now is second-date territory?'

Leaning forward, Daniel nudged his nose against the hair at her temple, breathing in lavender-scented shampoo. 'So when do you want to go out?'

There was a heavy sigh as her hands smoothed across his chest. 'We can't go on a date. We can barely manage a civil cup of coffee.'

'We just need to learn how to communicate better.'

Seemed to Daniel they were making some real headway in that department. He moved his nose to the other side of her temple and took another breath. The lavender wasn't having a calming effect on his body but the fact she was finding him hard to resist certainly seemed to be doing something to his sense of well-being.

She shook her head. 'We can't.'

'Making an effort not to bite each other's heads off might be a good place to start.'

'I meant *this*.'

'You don't mean that,' he said with conviction.

'Yes, I do.'

'No, you don't.'

'Yes, I do.' As he lifted his head she looked up at him from underneath her fringe. 'Could you stop acting like you know me better than I know myself?'

Considering she was no more able to keep her hands off him than he was to keep his off her, Daniel refused to back down. 'Would you have crossed the hall and kissed me?'

'No.'

'Do you regret that I crossed the hall to kiss you?' When she avoided his gaze and focused a small frown on his chest, he added, 'Remember, you suck at lying.'

'No,' she confessed reluctantly. 'I don't regret it.'

A step in the right direction…

She sighed again. 'But I should.'

And a step back…

Lifting the hand at her waist, he smoothed a strand of hair off her cheek. 'Tell me why.'

'There are at least a dozen reasons why we shouldn't be doing this.'

'I had ten on my list.'

She shot him a brief look of frustration. 'The very fact you even *have a list* should tell you I'm right.'

'I've been narrowing it down some.'

When she frowned, he brushed his thumb against her breast and felt her body respond to his touch.

'Danny, stop.'

He leaned in to nuzzle his nose into the hair above her ear. 'Do I need to remind you what I said about making things difficult for me when I want something?'

'There's no room in my life for involvement.'

'You forget you're talking to the guy who never stays in one place long enough for it to get complicated.' He brushed her hair off her shoulder to access her neck.

'I can't think when you're doing that.'

The breathless honesty made his mouth curve into a smile against her skin. *'Good.'*

'But we need to be sensible for a minute.' Her hands flattened against his chest and pushed.

Lifting his head so he could look into her eyes,

Daniel discovered the kind of steely determination that suggested he wasn't the only one she was resisting.

'Give me some space, Daniel. I mean it.'

The use of his full name made him frown.

'Please.'

A flash of vulnerability combined with the word she had never used around him before made him step back, but only as far as the opposite side of the door frame. Dropping his arms, he pushed his hands into the pockets of his jeans.

'I'm listening.'

'Don't do that,' she warned with a brief glare. 'If you want us to communicate better it has to start somewhere.'

'We were communicating fine until you started overthinking it.'

'We can't just jump into bed,' she protested.

'No?'

'No. Because to categorize it as friends with benefits we'd need to be friends in the first place and we're *not.'* When he opened his mouth she shook her head. 'I'm not done. Even if we were friends, we both know this is complicated.'

Number nine on his list, as it happened. Or was it eight? If it was eight, what was nine? While he tried to remember Jo continued listing the reasons they shouldn't get involved.

'Your sister is my best friend and your family—'

'What happens between us is no one's business but ours,' he replied in a tone that wouldn't accept any argument on the subject. 'We're consenting adults.'

'You're saying we sneak around and have secret sex?'

'There's a lot to recommend that one too.'

'I can't *lie* to your sister.'

'I didn't ask you to,' he said. 'I'm saying we see where this takes us before we complicate it with outside opinions.'

'We both know exactly where it will take us.'

'Sometimes these things are just a flash in the pan—burn hot, fizzle out fast.' But as the words left his mouth Daniel knew he didn't believe them. Once wouldn't be enough with her, just as one kiss hadn't been enough. After a second kiss he was ready for a third, a fourth and a fifth; preferably within the next few minutes. He wasn't looking for a commitment any more than she was. It wasn't something he could even begin to contemplate until he kicked his subconscious into line.

But spending what was left of his short lease with Jo suddenly felt like pretty good therapy to him.

Ignoring the warning in her eyes, he took a step forward. 'Can't hurt if we manage to communicate better, can it? If we follow this through to its natural conclusion, it'll be our decision. I'm not about to send out a mass email so people who know us can add their two cents. If you choose to tell Liv, that's up to you. Won't be you my family will come down on when we're done. It'll be me and I can handle that.'

'I won't be made out to be the victim of seduction.' She frowned. 'I'm a big girl. If something happens, it'll be on equal terms.'

'Wouldn't have it any other way.' He flashed a smile. 'All I'm doing is laying it out for you.'

She wavered. 'So we just try to communicate better and see what happens…'

'Exactly.'

'Knowing neither of us want to get involved…'

'You want no strings, I'm your man.' That she was getting closer to seeing things his way brought his hands out of his pockets. But as he lifted his arms she glanced down.

'What happened to your hand?' Frowning, she

took it in one of hers to study the damage more closely.

Daniel looked at the red scratches across the joints of his fingers and knuckles as if he'd forgotten they were there. He forgot a lot of things when he was kissing her.

'Scraped it on a wall,' he replied.

'Does it hurt?'

'No.' Not in the way she meant.

'Looks like it hurts,' she said in a low voice. 'Don't you wear gloves when you're working?'

'They got in the way.' It was as much as he was prepared to say on the subject. Turning his wrist, he threaded their fingers together, his free hand sliding under the hem of her blouse to touch the baby soft skin on her flank.

She trembled in response, long lashes growing heavy and another stuttered inward breath hauled through parted lips.

'I don't know what changed between us or why, but—'

'It's changed,' she finished. 'I know.'

'May as well explore it now it's here…'

Jo searched his eyes in the same way she had when she woke him up. It made him feel equally exposed, like standing in open ground without cover. Remaining still, he forced himself to endure the onslaught with more courage than last time. Her decision might ultimately rest on whether she found what she was looking for but he couldn't do much about that.

It was either there or it wasn't.

'You know I'm going to ask at some point.' She lowered her gaze to watch her palm flatten on his chest. She nodded. 'Just so you're ready for it next time…'

Daniel doubted he would ever be ready and was about to tell her it was a no-go area when she took a breath and confessed, 'I can't believe I'm even contemplating this…'

'It's not going anywhere,' he replied roughly.

'Hmm…' She pushed out her lower lip. 'Not till your lease is up.'

'Not till my lease is up.'

'Well, then,' she said softly as her fingers flexed against his sweater. 'If you're going to convince me to go against my better judgment you best get started.' The hand on his chest slid up around his neck, her gaze focused on his mouth. 'For the record, it could take a *lot* of persuasion.'

Daniel's head lowered. 'I can do persuasion.'

'We'll see…'

CHAPTER SEVEN

'I always thought creamy vanilla was the ice cream for me, but recently someone persuaded me to try some wild cherry. Oh, my, what have I been missing all these years?'

'CHEESE slice and a diet soda, please,' Jo said with a smile before she turned towards Daniel. 'Stubborn. Now you think of one word to describe me. And *be nice.*'

He reached a long arm across the heated glass cabinets to pay for their order. 'Because calling me stubborn was supposed to be a compliment?'

'You're saying you aren't?'

'I prefer to call it determination.'

'Admit when you're wrong a little more often, it *could* be called determination,' she allowed, adding an innocent flutter of her lashes when he glanced at her.

'I can admit when I'm wrong.'

'Can you do it out loud?'

When he took a long breath, Jo bit her lip to stifle a chuckle. While the back-and-forth between them hadn't changed all that much, it was less sharp than it had been before. Both of them putting more effort into it helped, as did Daniel's newfound ability to know when she was teasing him instead of taunting him. But there were times she still wondered how long it could last.

'Your turn,' she prompted. It was met with a long enough moment of consideration to merit a sigh. 'Can't think of a word that isn't an insult, can you?'

'I can think of several words that aren't insults after the last few days.' A smile hovered at the corners of his mouth. 'Move closer and I'll whisper them to you.'

'Do I have to remind you why we're in a public place?' She waved an encouraging hand between them. 'Work with me here.'

If all it took to remove any remaining doubts from her mind were the constant reminders of why they were trying to communicate better, they'd have been eating in. Knowing what she did of his wicked streak, quite possibly off each other's bodies. But since the night they had their elevator argument, Jo had been ignoring the small voice inside her head: the one that still thought where they were headed was a huge mistake. When he wasn't there it was louder. Then she would lie in the darkness, hear him on the other side of the wall, and the only thing she could think about when she saw him again was making him feel better. Granted, it made *her* feel better too, but it still hadn't silenced the voice.

'Fearless.'

She blinked. 'What?'

'You wanted a word I'd use to describe you.' Taking their order with a nod of thanks, he turned towards the door. 'There you go.'

'That's how you see me?'

'What's wrong with it?'

Apart from the fact he couldn't be more wrong? 'It's a compliment,' she replied.

'Underestimating me again?' Holding the door open, Daniel lowered his voice as she walked past him. 'Being bad isn't the only thing I'm good at.'

Jo ignored the hum of delight whispering over her body when she thought about how very good he was at being bad. She could hold a conversation with him without thinking about sex every five minutes. She darn well could!

'No one's fearless,' she announced. 'Everyone's

afraid of something; by overcoming it they earn the word brave.'

He adjusted his longer stride to hers when they hit the sidewalk. 'What are you afraid of?'

'Oh, no,' she laughed. 'I'm not falling for that one. I say spiders, you'll start a collection.'

'Might consider one of those big hairy guys you keep in a glass case. I heard they're a low-maintenance pet.' He smiled when she shuddered. 'One word wasn't enough to begin with. If I had two I'd have said fearless and wary.'

'Isn't that an oxymoron?'

'You think I don't know what that means.'

'Word-of-the-day calendars can be very educational.'

'I have another one: manicured and mischievous.'

'Careful, Danny.' She smiled. 'It's starting to sound like you've put some thought into this before today.'

'Tornado in high heels, that's another one...'

Despite the fact she liked everything he'd come up with so far, Jo tutted. 'Little too far over the word-count now.'

'Your turn again. And after you laid stubborn

on me, try harder. I might bruise easier than you think.'

When they stopped at a crossing she took her time picking another word. Had to be careful his ego didn't engulf Texas and try to take over the world, didn't she? Mentally crossing out every-thing pre-communicate-better-days too—*which might take a while*—she gently swayed the skirt that lent itself to the motion. Theme of the day was vintage and the black and white striped fif-ties dress was the most 'her' she had felt since she started the challenge. It was a much-needed reminder of what her life had been like before ev-erything changed so fast it felt as if her feet had barely touched the ground.

'Can't stop doing that, can you?' he asked.

'Doing what?'

'The thing you're doing with your skirt.'

Rocking her hips a little more, she brightened. 'Is it bothering you?'

'No. Just wondered if you knew you were doing it.'

She shrugged. 'It's a fun dress.'

'And now I'm wondering if you still leave out cookies and a glass of milk for the jolly fat guy in red.'

Despite the obvious amusement in his eyes, Jo felt the need to defend what for her was an ethos for life. 'If you don't make time for fun every now and again the big, bad things can be harder to take.'

'Are you saying I don't know how to have fun?'

From the well of memories she had chosen to forget she sought one that associated Daniel with the kind of fun things she attached to his three brothers. She had dozens of memories of them tossing a football and joshing around but Daniel, not so much. What did he do with his time apart from work, a daily run and utilizing every tool in the seduction toolbox to turn her into a boneless heap of wanton woman?

'Define your idea of "fun" for me,' she demanded as they entered Washington Square Park and she looked up at the iconic arch modelled after the Arc de Triomphe in Paris.

If he asked she would tell him eating lunch close to its shadow was one of her favorite fun things to do, especially on a day like the one they were experiencing. Spiffed up to its former glory, with a backdrop of clear blue sky. She'd stare up at it and imagine she was sitting by the original.

She made the same vow every time she saw it: *Soon.*

Since she was moving up the magazine's short-list each year, she felt closer than ever to fulfilling the promise.

When she looked at Daniel and found innuendo glinting in his eyes, she felt the usual response skim through her veins and tighten her abdomen. But that wasn't what she'd meant. 'I mean outside of adult fun. What do you do to relax when you're not working?'

'Run, train, gym time; long hours dedicated to maintaining the level of fitness you finally got round to noticing...'

He cut loose his infamous smile, *on her.*

Wow. That thing really did pack a punch up close.

She had forgotten that. But since the memory of the last time he unleashed it on her was buried so deep there must have been a very good reason for forgetting it, Jo decided not to go digging. 'Toss a football in the park, play practical jokes on the guys in your unit or meet up with friends for a beer...' She lifted her brows. 'When's the last time you did anything like that?'

'We tossed a football in camp when I was overseas. Not much else to do when we weren't being shot at.'

She didn't get how he could be so blasé about his time there when it was obvious whatever happened still tortured him. The subject of his nightmares was one they'd avoided but maybe…in the bright light of day…while they were getting along better…

'Not like my inbox was overflowing with emails, was it?' he asked before she could find a place to start.

Jo shook her head. 'You didn't want to hear from me.'

'You'd be surprised the difference an email can make to a Marine in a war zone. I saw guys go for days on the smile they got hearing from folks they barely knew in high school.' His gaze swept the surrounding area for a place to sit before he laid a large palm against the small of her back to guide her. 'It's a reminder of home. Some guys needed that.'

'Did you?'

'My problem was never remembering.' He frowned.

The unspoken *'it's trying to forget'* made Jo's

voice soften in response. 'You're not a machine, Danny.'

'There are times it would be a lot easier if I was.'

'You say the stupidest things sometimes.' But as they approached an available bench she wondered what she'd have done if she'd thought an email made a difference to him back then. Even if it was from someone he hadn't liked. 'If I'd known I'd have written.' She smiled up at him. 'You'd have got *War & Peace* on everyday life in Manhattan.'

'With daily tips for the fashion-conscious Marine…?'

'I heard it's all about the camouflage this season.'

'I'll think about letting you write next time I go.'

'You're going again?'

'Not likely to happen soon,' he said in a tone that suggested he was disappointed. 'There's three months left on my papers before I decide whether to re-up.'

'You've already decided, haven't you?'

'Once a Marine, always a Marine.'

Jo frowned at how little she liked the idea of him being overseas again. She might not have lost sleep over it last time, but she knew she would now. 'You're a cop too. Doesn't that mean anything?'

'I've been both for a long time.'

'I know, but it's like you're married to the Marines and fooling around with the NYPD on the side.'

'I don't fool around,' he said seriously.

If he thought it was something she needed to hear, it wasn't necessary. Any relationship she'd heard he had might not have lasted long, but she couldn't remember there ever being a suggestion he was fooling around. He wasn't the kind of guy who cheated on a woman. It was part of the Brannigan loyalty and honour code.

'Kinda feels like you're more faithful to one than the other,' she pointed out in relation to his work. 'Semper Fi, that's the motto, right?'

'Ooh-rah,' he replied in a low rumble, smiling when she rolled her eyes. 'The Marines are my first love. You never forget that. Being a cop is different. It's a marriage that was arranged for me before I was born.'

'You didn't want to be a cop?'

'Let's just say it took a while to find my niche.'

Since she'd always assumed all of the Brannigans had the same calling, Jo was surprised. But if he'd loved it so much, 'Why did you leave the Marines?'

'I didn't.'

'You switched to the Reserves and came home.'

'Things change.'

'Do you regret it?' she asked as she sat down.

'Not on the good days,' he replied.

It seemed a tad ironic to Jo she had accused him of not knowing her when she was discovering so many things she hadn't known about him. Usually she liked to think she swayed towards giving people the benefit of the doubt. But with Daniel there had always been a wall of distrust; one they built higher and wider every time their paths crossed. She was still wary of him but that was understandable. Trust wasn't built overnight.

As he turned to hand over the pizza box, she looked into his eyes and saw a hint of shadow. Experiencing an immediate pang of regret, she tried to lighten the mood. 'I've decided I'm giving you a relaxation make-over.'

'If it involves bubble baths and scented candles you can forget it.'

Curling her fingers, she punched him in the upper arm to even up the score for the sucker punch of his infamous smile. 'Don't mock what you haven't tried.'

Daniel glanced at his arm as she shook her hand. 'Been wanting to do that for years, haven't you?'

'You have *no idea.*' Unfortunately, now she knew who would come out of it worse, it wasn't an option any more.

Reaching out, he captured her hand and ran his thumb over the rise and fall of her knuckles. As he repeated the caress heat rushed up her arm in waves. That part she'd almost gotten used to. What she found harder to handle was the message she could read in his eyes as he did it. At first she'd thought it was her imagination. Then, as it was with everything between them of late, she chalked it up to one of the numerous sexual messages he silently transmitted to her. It had been easier to think of it that way. But in the sunlight—the vivid blue of his eyes bright enough to put the sky to shame—it felt like something more.

I'll take care of you, it said.

Jo didn't like it. She didn't need him to take care of her. She could take care of herself.

Holding her gaze hostage, he did something un-expected and bowed his head to place a kiss on the skin he'd caressed. Jo watched, mesmerized, as his chin lifted and he smiled.

Seriously, where had *this* Danny been hiding for the last five and a half years?

'Let me know if you need anywhere else kissed better...'

'Well, that's a shame.' She sighed and reached into the box for her slice of pizza. 'Opportunities to be gallant are rare in this day and age. And you just blew yours.'

When there was a chuckle of deep laughter, she turned her head to study the effect it had on his face. Mocking amusement she was used to; the glint in his eyes that hinted he knew something she didn't and his enjoyment was at her expense, she knew all too well. But the way it relaxed some of the tension around his eyes, suggesting he'd experienced a moment of the kind of fun he obviously needed thanks to *her*?

Well, as it happened, it felt pretty darn good.

She was smiling back at him when her phone rang. Digging in one of the pockets of her skirt to retrieve it, she checked the number and frowned. *Darn it.* Not now.

'Hi, Stu... No, I appreciate it.' She glanced at Daniel from the corner of her eye. 'Can you try and keep him there for me? Thanks.' Pushing the phone back in her pocket, she dropped the pizza into the box and wiped her hand with the napkin. 'I have to go.'

'I'm coming with you.'

Yes, she'd thought he might say that. While he could catch her off guard with some things, in others he was as predictable as queues for the Empire State Building. She shook her head, 'It's your day off. You're going to do something fun.'

'It took two days and a late night for you to free up time in your schedule,' he pointed out. 'Your idea of what we did with it may have differed from mine, but the general idea was to spend it together.'

'I know,' Jo replied with another pang of regret.

He had been remarkably patient in regard to her schedule versus his shift pattern. Discussing it made her realize the number of times he would have to sacrifice much-needed sleep to see her. For a second it made her resent the intrusion of the present by the past a little more than usual. But he had been right about what he could see in her eyes the night he surprised her in the hall. For one month out of every twelve, she was resigned to doing what she had to do.

Leaning forward, she placed a quick kiss on a clean-shaven cheek before standing up. 'I promise to make it up to you when I get back.'

'Nice try.' He stood up with her. 'I'll drive you there. It'll be quicker.'

Not in Manhattan traffic, it wouldn't. 'I know what you're doing and it's not that I—'

Taking a step forward, he laid a hand on the wide red belt at her waist, his voice low. 'Are we headed for an argument?'

'I don't want us to be,' Jo confessed.

Avoiding his gaze, she brushed an invisible piece of lint off his jersey with the backs of her fingers. No matter how addictive it had become, she liked being able to touch him. She liked the heat she could feel through his clothes, the solidness of his presence. But since she couldn't get used to him being there, she lowered her arm.

'Sooner we go, sooner we can be back,' he said firmly.

When he took her hand and turned them around, Jo tried to find a way to get out of it. The idea of him taking a deeper step into her old world than he already had sent a chill down her spine. Jack was the key to a door she didn't want to open.

Behind it was the old Jo, the invisible girl who

had been lonely and lost. Despite the need she had for it, Jo knew the risk associated with accepting help. She had watched the effect it had on some of her peers; how well-meaning people with good intentions could begin to make decisions for them until they didn't have control over their lives any more. With hindsight the new Jo supposed it wasn't *that* dissimilar to the battle for independence teenagers fought everywhere. But in the present it felt like a much-needed reminder not to lean on a man like Daniel, even for a moment.

Huge mistake, the little voice repeated.

Something dangerously close to panic crossed her chest as his truck came into sight. Glancing down the street, she saw the sign for the subway station. Looking at his truck again, she frowned at the idea of an argument. The phrase 'rock and a hard place' jumped into her head.

'Danny...' When they stopped to cross the street, she tried to reclaim her hand. 'I—'

'I know you don't want me to go with you.' Tightening his fingers, he turned to face her. 'But if you want me to bend a little from time to time, you have to do a little bending of your own. You know that, don't you?'

Oh, he was *good*. Negotiation 101 obviously

hadn't been lost on him during the NYPD training. He knew exactly the tone of deep, rough rumble to use on her, had enough sincerity in his eyes
to make her feel she was letting him down if she
didn't make an effort. She frowned at his chest
again. If it was something other than Jack she
could try to bend, but—

'Look at me, Jo.'

With a blink, she obeyed.

'We're good right now, aren't we?'

She nodded. They were. It was another part of
the reason she didn't want to take him with her.

'So we go in, you do whatever you need to do,
and then we get to enjoy the rest of our day.'

It sounded so simple when he put it like that.

Nudging the tip of his nose against hers, he angled his head and placed a kiss on the corner of
her mouth. 'I can think of at least a half-dozen
fun things we can do when we get back...'

Eyelids growing heavy, Jo smiled as he placed
another kiss on the other corner of her mouth. She
knew what he was doing but while the rest of the
world disappeared around them she could feel her
resistance melting away.

'You have a one-track mind,' she mumbled as
he changed the angle of his head.

'There's a reason for that.'

Slanting his mouth over hers, he spent several minutes persuading her to go against her better judgment. She might have issued the challenge after their elevator argument but if she knew how well he could do it...

He lifted his head, long fingers flexed around hers, his alert gaze sweeping over the traffic while she stared at him.

If she could just figure out what it was that hadn't been there before. What made her see him differently and want him so much the memories of all the times they argued faded into the distance...

'Let's go, babe.'

CHAPTER EIGHT

'The jacket you never wore? The jeans you swore you'd get back into one day? Sometimes you have to be firm about the things you keep and the things you let go.'

JO LEANED across the wooden bar to greet the man in front of the optics with a kiss above his greying beard.

'Well, aren't you a picture?' he said with a smile.

Taking a step back, she placed her hands on either side of her waist and struck a pose. 'You like?'

'I do.'

The sound of laughter pulled her gaze to the other side of the room as her hands dropped. 'How far are we in?'

Daniel noticed the change in her voice; as if it was a question she had asked a hundred times but already knew the answer. He stored the information away with her reaction to the phone call. The change in her then had been immediate too. One minute he was sitting next to bright, full-of-life, sassy, sexy Jo and the next it was like sitting next to a shell. At the time it had felt as if something were stolen from him.

Daniel had resented the hell out of that.

'Coming up on three hours,' the man replied.

Jo glanced to her side. 'Sorry.' She waved a hand, 'Daniel, meet Stu. Stu, meet Daniel.'

They shook hands across the bar.

'First time she's brought anyone with her in ten years,' Stu said with a smile. 'Can I get you anything?'

Daniel shook his head. 'Designated driver.'

'Better order something if you're staying.' Jo looked across the room again. 'This could take a while.'

As she walked away, Stu explained, 'It's in the timing. She takes him home too early, he finds his way back. If not here, it's somewhere else.'

Nodding as if he'd already known, he watched her father greet her with an arm around tight, narrow shoulders before making introductions. Immediately Daniel wanted to scoop her up and take her back to where they were before the call came. But he had to treat it as a recon mission.

With that in mind he'd let her handle Jack her way, *for now.*

'You could try barring him,' he said dryly.

When he looked at Stu again, he discovered he was being studied with caution. 'Jo said she'd prefer to get a phone call than spend time searching for him.'

'It's good to know she has people who will do that,' he replied with sincerity.

The older man visibly relaxed. 'Used to be more of us, but bars change hands over the years.'

When Jo returned, she lifted her chin a very visible inch before looking Daniel in the eye. 'Is there any point telling you to go home?'

'No,' he replied.

'Figures.' She flashed another smile at Stu. 'I'll take one of your famous coffees if there's a pot on the go.'

'Is the designated driver sure he doesn't want one?'

'He takes his black.'

'I'll bring them over.'

They were sitting in a corner booth when Daniel broached the subject with, 'How many bar owners have your phone number?'

'Danny—'

'It's just a question.'

'No, it's not.' She sighed heavily. 'It's an opening to an argument. Don't make me regret bringing you here.'

Stu arrived with their coffees. As he watched him return to the bar Daniel lowered his voice. 'I'm not going to argue with you.'

'I'm glad to hear it.'

'But I'm not going to stay silent.'

'If what you have to say involves a lecture on how to handle Jack you can forget it. I've been doing this for a long time. I don't need your help.' She reached for her coffee and took a sip.

When she glanced across the bar as she set her cup down, Daniel lifted his hand. Sliding it beneath a curtain of silky hair, he wrapped his fingers around her neck, soothing tense muscles with a firm, circular movement. It took a minute, but eventually her head became heavy against his forefinger.

'*Mmm*, that feels good.'

Ignoring the reaction from his body to the low moan, he smiled. 'Magic fingers…'

'And I didn't even have to put coins in the slot.'

'You can pay me later.'

The brief smile his comment earned faded as

she glanced across the bar again. 'It's not that there aren't some things I'm fine talking about...'

'So start there.'

'...but before I do I want your word you won't interfere.' With a blink of long lashes, her gaze tangled with his. 'I mean it, Danny. No advice, no leaflets for places I can get help and when we leave here we don't talk about it again.'

'I'm not the first person you've said that to.'

'You're not the first *Brannigan* I've said it to.' She shrugged a shoulder. 'Liv tried to get involved once.'

If she hadn't, they would have had words. Considering she only tried *once*, it was still tempting. But if he opened his mouth in Jo's defence his sister would know something was up. She could be intuitive that way.

He took a short breath. 'I can't give you my word—'

'Then we're not talking about it.'

'I'm not done.' He moved his fingers to ease the returning tension in her neck. 'Learning to communicate better after so many years of arguing was never going to be easy. If blunt is what it takes from time to time then—'

She arched a brow. 'You know I'm going to remind you of this when it's your turn, don't you?'

The fingers on her neck stilled. She didn't know
he had no intention of talking to her about his
nightmares. If he hadn't been likely to talk about
them before, spending time with her had made
him twice as determined. He didn't want the darkness of his subconscious to intrude on what was
rapidly becoming a haven. He dropped his arm
to his side.

'I shouldn't have said that,' she said with regret.
'I knew this would happen. I should have listened
to the voice that told me—'

'What we're doing is still a huge mistake?'

A hint of astonishment mixed with a sparkle of
anger in her eyes. 'Not what I was going to say.'

'Tell me I'm wrong.'

'What's happening between us has nothing to
do with this,' she argued.

Putting together what she said with his thoughts
on the subject of discussing his nightmares, Daniel
realized, 'You don't let your old life cross over
into the new one and vice versa, right?'

'Not if I can help it,' she admitted.

'How's that working out for you?'

'Was going pretty well...'

'Until me…'

Her expression softened. 'Until you…'

Reaching out, his fingers sought the knots of tension at the base of her neck again. 'Start with something simple. Tell me how you met Stu.'

Louder laughter pulled her gaze across the room while she considered what to tell him. Judging by the brief frown on her face, it wasn't that simple.

'I was fourteen,' she said in a low voice. 'Figured if I couldn't stop him drinking, I'd make it more difficult. I went to all the bars within an eight-block radius to see where he'd run up tabs. Deal was, they'd stop giving him credit and I'd pay them off a few dollars a week. The ones who gave me most trouble, I paid first. The patient ones— guys like Stu—would take less on weeks I found it tough.' She took a breath. 'Took two part-time jobs and a few years, but I got there. Even made a few friends along the way…'

Earning their respect as she did it, Daniel surmised. He would have liked to have met her back then. But while fourteen-year-old Jo had been surviving the Urban Jungle, a twenty-year-old Daniel was in theatre with the Marines. He could imagine what she would have thought of him if she'd met him before he'd signed up at eighteen. He was a loose gun then; the kind of guy who was more trouble than he was worth. Looking back, he knew he would have had more respect for her than he had for himself.

'Did it slow him down?' he asked.

'No.' She shook her head. 'It forced him outside the eight-block radius. That's when he started disappearing.'

Daniel's fingers stilled again. 'He's the reason you were homeless when Liv met you.'

She shrugged as if it didn't matter. 'I couldn't make the rent. He disappeared when we were already on shaky ground with the landlord. When I knew I couldn't hold out I scouted around for some place dry close to school, packed what I could carry and left. The rest you know.'

Anger flared inside him. 'Why didn't you ask for help? There are people out there who—'

'I was eighteen,' she said with a glare of warning. 'I could take care of myself. All I needed was a few weeks to finish high school and get my diploma.'

Fingers moving, his gaze slid across the bar to acquire a new target. What kind of man did that to his kid? Why was she still taking care of him?

'Where was your mother?' he asked.

Her neck stiffened. 'She died.'

'When?'

'Accident when I was eight.'

'What happened?'

'Hit and run on her way back from the local store.'

He remembered her saying something about Jack being worse one month out of twelve. 'The anniversary of her death is this month, isn't it?'

'Yes.' Leaning forward to reach for her cup, Jo dislodged his hand with a subtle shrug of her shoulders. 'And we're done talking about this now.'

Daniel's gaze slid back to his target. He knew exactly who he was talking to next. Five minutes should do it. But before he went looking for a window of opportunity he had to ask the question he didn't want to ask.

'Was he ever violent with you?'

'Don't—'

'I need to know.'

The rough tone of his voice turned her head, her gaze searching his eyes before her expression softened. 'He's not that kind of drunk. Jack gets happy. That's half the problem. People buy him drinks 'cos he's such a fun guy to be around.'

When laughter sounded she smiled ruefully. 'See what I mean?'

'You were lucky,' Daniel replied, when what he really meant was *Jack* was lucky.

'Yes,' Jo said dryly. 'I spent every waking moment of my adolescence being eternally grateful for the fact my father is an alcoholic.'

Despite thinking it was the most honest thing she'd said on the subject, Daniel shook his head. 'Not what I meant.'

The unexpected touch of a fine-boned hand on his thigh drew a sharp hiss of breath through his lips. His thoughts stuttered to a standstill. As always every muscle in his body jerked in response, searing heat seeping into his veins and thickening his blood.

'I know what you meant,' she said in an intimate voice. 'But you don't have to worry about me.'

Daniel disagreed. Way he saw it, while they were together she was *his* to take care of and *his* to protect.

'He would never hurt me,' she reassured him.

'Would he know if he knocked you over or if you injured yourself carrying him upstairs?' He clamped her hand to his thigh when she tried to remove it. 'How about when you have to clean up after him or when you're losing sleep worrying where he is? Not every bruise is visible.'

'If you don't stop that I'm going to make you leave.'

She could *try*.

'I'm not going to pretend I don't care.'

'Did I ask you to?' She frowned. 'But what you have to remember is this isn't because it's me, Danny. You're *that guy*: the one who feels he has to make a difference.'

'Don't make me out to be a hero.' If she knew him better she would know how woefully short he fell of the definition.

'Then stop trying to be one.' When a second attempt at freeing her hand didn't get her anywhere, she shook her head. 'I don't need you to rescue me. I need you to trust I know what I'm doing and believe I have my reasons for doing it.'

'Tell me what they are.'

As she tore her gaze from his a pained expression crossed her face. 'I don't want to have a fight with you. But if you keep doing this I won't be able to stop it happening.'

'You give me one good reason why you keep doing this and I'll back off.'

'Why do you need to know?' She jerked her

brows. 'And don't say it's part of the whole communicating-better thing because this has nothing to do with us.'

'This is a prime example of you not making it easy for people to get to know you,' Daniel replied flatly.

'Getting to know me better isn't high on your list of priorities when you're trying to get me into bed.'

'If it wasn't we'd already have shared a bed.'

'You say that like I don't have a choice.'

'Tell me you don't want me.' When something close to a growl sounded in the back of her throat, he leaned closer. 'I can tell you how much I want you. You're never out of my head. I've spent dozens of hours thinking about the places I want to kiss you and the things I want to do to you. I want to explore every inch of your body, discover all the hidden places you never even knew you had. I want to drive you so crazy that if I don't take you, we'll both go insane. I want—'

'*Stop,*' she breathed.

'Tell me you don't want me.'

Her eyes darkened. 'You know I do.'

'If I get to know you better, the experience will be better for both of us. You have my word on that.'

She blinked. 'You're very good at this.'

The statement lifted the corners of his mouth. 'Only when I think it's worth the effort.'

'I won't fall for you,' she said firmly.

Daniel shook his head. 'I don't want you to.'

With another blink, she lifted her chin. 'No falling for me either.'

His smile grew. 'Okay.'

'One reason I keep doing this…'

'Just one.' He nodded, silently adding another *for now.*

'Coney Island.'

Daniel wondered if there would ever be a time she didn't surprise him. 'Am I supposed to know what that means?'

'No,' she replied. 'But I can explain it.' She stared into the air beside his head and took a short breath. 'I was ten or eleven. Jack quit drinking for long enough to remember he had a kid and we went to Coney Island for a day.' Her mouth curled into a wistful smile. 'We went on every ride, ate cotton candy and corn dogs until I felt sick and it was one of the best days of my life.'

When her gaze met his, he caught a glimpse of sweet and vulnerable woman at odds with her usual sass and confidence. Something he didn't recognize expanded in his chest, filling the cavity and making it difficult to breathe.

'That's one of the reasons I keep doing this,' she said with a shrug of a shoulder. 'Because I still remember Coney Island and the day I got my dad back.'

As she avoided his gaze Daniel wrapped his arms around her and pulled her close. She nestled her head in the curve between his neck and shoulder. When he felt the warmth of her breath against his skin a wave of protectiveness washed over him, tightening his hold. In response she relaxed with a sigh, which gave him the impression what he had done held more value than anything he could have said. But when she looked up at him and smiled tremulously, the something he hadn't recognized shifted inside his chest again and Daniel sensed trouble. He brushed her hair back from her cheek, focusing on the movement as he bought time to seek out the source of the danger.

Trouble was, she might think she liked living on the edge, but she didn't know how sharp it could be if a person stood on it for long enough. The question had never been *when* he would fall, it was always *where*: one side heaven, the other hell.

He had visited the latter too often over the years. It shouldn't have been a surprise he wanted to reach out and grab a taste of the alternative, even if it was just for a while. But hold on to it for too long and there was a chance he might haul her into the abyss with him, clinging desperately to whatever light he could find in the darkness. It was why he could never ask for something from her that he couldn't return. Risking his life was easier than emotional involvement. When the stakes were at their highest he felt more alive, stronger; free of the things that weighed him down. It was how he felt when he kissed her.

Oh, yeah, he was in trouble all right.

To make matters worse, she angled her chin, her expression suggesting she knew something was wrong.

Daniel took a short breath, 'How much longer do you think we'll be here?'

She glanced across the bar. 'An hour, maybe two…' She looked at him again. 'If you want to go—'

'No,' he said firmly. 'I was just thinking we skipped lunch and you should eat. If Stu can't rustle up a sandwich, I'll go get us something.'

Releasing her, he slid around the booth and

walked away. While there were certain things he couldn't give her, he liked to think he could make up for it in other ways. He wanted to take care of her. Not out of a sense of duty attached to his job or the responsibility that stemmed from her connection to his family. Strangely enough it wasn't entirely because she meant something to him, though there was no denying she did. When he thought it over, it kept coming back to one thing. The same thing that had made him retreat when he thought he might hurt her and try to make amends when it felt as if he had.

She was *Jo*.

It was as simple and as complicated as that.

CHAPTER NINE

'There's a lot of truth in the sayings on a fridge magnet. For example: How many roads must a man walk down before he'll admit he's lost?'

HE WAS driving her just the tiniest bit crazy.

'Could you quit doing that?' She slapped his hand.

'Isn't clearing up after dinner usually one of the things a guy gets brownie points for doing?'

'I could be a closet neat freak for all you know.'

Glancing around her apartment, he had the gall to look amused. 'Can't be easy in Aladdin's cave...'

Considering every eclectic knick-knack, photo frame and somewhat haphazard arrangement of soft furnishings was a much-loved memento of the life he had turned upside down, Jo took offence. 'People who live in an apartment for longer than a handful of months have been known to make it look like home.'

Daniel leaned back against the counter. 'Apparently they also make friends with everyone inside two blocks. You should be more careful when you live alone. Think about varying your routine. The guy in the Chinese place knew your name and where you lived from your order.'

'Traditionally that's how food gets delivered,' Jo said dryly as she folded down the edges of the cartons.

'Not when an order is being collected.'

'Do you see potential serial killers everywhere you look?' She frowned at how snippy she sounded. 'I trust in my initial impression of people. There tends to be truth in it until our heads get in the way. You should try it some time.'

'You know I'm going to ask the obvious now, right?'

'Not going there.'

'I can take it.'

'Not my main concern.'

'It's because it opens us up to my initial impression of you, isn't it?' He opened the refrigerator door. 'You telling me you're not curious?'

Placing the cartons on a shelf, she turned to take their glasses to the sink. 'It's got nothing to do with curiosity. I doubt you even remember when it was.'

'I have a long memory.'

She sighed. 'Revisiting the things that started us arguing in the first place probably isn't wise at this point.'

'Can't be any worse than the mood you've been in since I got here. When you're ready to tell me what the problem is let me know.' Closing the door, he pushed his large hands into the pockets of his jeans and continued the conversation as if he hadn't made her feel like a petulant three-year-old. 'We met the fourth of July weekend Liv brought you home.'

No, they didn't. If she was in a better mood than the one she'd been in since *before* he got there, she could have told him exactly when they met. It was—

Lifting her chin, she blinked as the memory made its way up from the deepest recesses of the well where she stored the things she'd chosen to forget. Suddenly she could remember the first time he sucker-punched her with his infamous smile. She could see what he was wearing, how gorgeous he looked, most of all she remembered how she'd *felt*. It didn't take a genius to work out the events between their first and second meeting had an effect too. But it certainly shed a different light on her reaction to him when he foolishly opened his mouth that fourth of July weekend.

'You were quieter then,' he said.

'Bit difficult to get a word in edgeways when your family is gathered en masse.' Setting the glass on the drainer with a shaking hand, she took several calming breaths.

'Roomful of cops is normally enough for most people.'

She nodded. 'There was that too.'

'Shouldn't be a problem unless you feel guilty...'

Grimacing, Jo reminded herself he couldn't possibly know what she currently felt guilty about. Instead she thought back to her feelings that day. 'Bit hard to avoid guilt when you're somewhere you know you don't belong.'

'That's how you felt?'

'I didn't belong anywhere back then.'

'What about now?'

'I like to think I've claimed my own little corner of the world. You should try that some time too.'

'You think I haven't?' he asked as she turned to face him.

Jo avoided his too-blue gaze when it felt as if he

could see right through her mask of calm. 'The big pile of unpacked boxes in your apartment would suggest otherwise.'

'Short lease, remember?'

That big ticking clock she could hear? The one telling her how little time she had to repair the damage inflicted by the war *she'd* started? Oh, yes, she remembered. Since it sped up the count-down, it added to the regret she felt for taking the assignment she was offered that afternoon.

Daniel had started texting her when she was in the office preparing for an editorial meeting. Initially a continuation of the word game they'd played—one she didn't intend to play while they were *working*—she ended up grinning like an idiot by the time they were swapping comments chock-a-block with sexual innuendo. He really was *bad*. An hour later the girls sitting at the desks next to her demanded to know who 'he' was because it had to be a man to put a smile like *that* on her face. They asked for details and it was tempting to share them, if for no other reason than she hadn't been able to with anyone else.

She was dangerously close to blushing—and she had *never* blushed—when her editor appeared, sent everyone scurrying back to work and asked if she could have a moment. To make matters worse the epitome of unabashedly single, career-driven woman felt the need to enquire about her 'availability' for a big assignment before offering it to her. As a result the words 'yes' and 'absolutely' left Jo's lips before she had time to consider exactly what it meant.

When looking around her apartment led to thoughts of how much she would miss it when she was gone, she frowned. 'Don't you want a place you can call home?'

'New York is home, doesn't matter where I live in it.'

Jo disagreed. She had lived in the city her entire life, but since four weeks of that time had involved sleeping beneath an underpass she knew the difference between living somewhere and having a place to call home. She looked into his eyes again. 'What is it about here you like best?'

He thought about it for a moment. 'You work in New York, you see people face to face. It's not like California where you spend half your life in a car or overseas when you fight an enemy without ever looking into their eyes.'

It was the kind of insight that would have made

her like him a lot earlier if she'd given him half a chance. 'When were you in California?'

'I was stationed in San Diego with the Marines.'

Another thing she hadn't known. 'You said work in New York. What is it you like about living here?'

'Same answer.'

'Nothing else?'

'You could try telling me what you're looking for,' he replied with a hint of a smile.

A lump appeared in her throat, forcing her to take a moment and swallow it so she could control her voice. She didn't deserve a smile. Not when she'd been the way she was with him since he landed at her door. It wasn't his fault her head was a mess. Not *entirely*. 'I don't get how you can see here as home without looking for a few hundred square feet to call your own. Aren't you sick of living out of boxes?'

'You forget up until not so long ago those boxes were in storage. Everything I needed I carried on my back.'

'Everything a *Marine* needed,' she clarified. 'You're home now, so why not make one? You can't tell me after the number of times you've moved apartments there haven't been places you liked enough to stay.'

'There were.'

'Then why do you…?' Her voice trailed off as some of the pieces slotted together. 'You move because of the nightmares, don't you? The minute someone hears you or you *think* they've heard you…' She knew instinctively she was right but it didn't make sense. He'd been moving from place to place for as long as she'd known him. She took a short breath. 'I'm just gonna jump right in here…'

'Do you have another speed?'

'Did something happen when you were overseas?'

'It's not the first time you've asked that question.' His eyes narrowed. 'What makes you so sure something happened?'

'If it didn't where do the nightmares come from?'

'How about we try to forget I have them?'

'Go back to pretending I don't know?' Her eyes widened in disbelief. 'Can you even *do* that?'

'Works better if you don't bring it up.'

'How long have you had them?'

The desire she felt to give him what he'd been

searching for returned with the shadows in his eyes. There was no point denying it. Since the first night she heard him yelling beyond the wall, it had felt as if he were calling out to her. Now, if she could take his pain and give him even one night of peace, she would do it for him. Any secrets he wanted to stay hidden she would keep safe, tucked away with one she already carried for him. But when it came to anything more, she couldn't see past a sudden crippling fear of falling for him.

Using every trick she had learnt in the past to hide how she really felt, she lifted her chin. 'What happened to trying to communicate better?'

'The theory behind that was we wouldn't argue as much.' He smirked. 'In case you hadn't got it by now, pushing me on this will have the opposite effect.'

'If having an argument is what it takes to get you to talk to me then we're about to have one.'

'We both know you've been itching to pick a fight with me since I got here.'

The sensation he was backing off again wasn't helping. She *hated* when he did that. Frustration bubbled inside her. 'How long, Daniel?'

'And now I'm Daniel again.' Taking his hands

out of his pockets, he pushed off the counter and headed for the chair where he'd tossed his jacket. 'How about I go back into the hall and we try starting tonight over again?'

Jo followed him. 'Whether you like it or not we've been in these nightmares together since you moved in.'

'Now you're using guilt to get me to talk to you?' His fingers closed around his jacket. 'Keep this up and we'll go from communicating better to name, rank and serial number.'

'Do you have any idea how difficult it is to hear you in that much pain?' She frowned as the truth left her lips. 'I spend half the night waiting for it to start and when it does it's *hell*.'

When he clammed up in a way that suggested he had never intended to talk about it, Jo wanted to slap him. Knowing she would have equal difficulty discussing certain things didn't seem to make a difference. She just wanted to help or offer comfort or simply listen while he talked it through. Not to feel so cut off from him when they suddenly had so little time left.

'Yesterday you wanted one reason why I still help Jack. Now I'm asking you for an answer.' Taking a breath, Jo vowed it was the last time she would bend unless he bent a little in return. It was uncomfortable, not to mention a little scary, being out on a limb alone. *'How long?'*

She didn't think she could get into an argument without other things spilling out in the heat of the moment. Things she wasn't ready to talk about yet, if ever. Avoiding his icy gaze, she pointed across the room. 'I'll be over there on the sofa while you decide whether to stay or go.'

It was as much leeway as she could give him. His refusal to talk to her about the nightmares after she'd talked to him about her past felt like a rejection. What was worse, it *hurt*. She should have kept her mouth shut, had no idea why she had confided in him in the first place, and if the first time she shared things with someone ended with her feeling like a fool…

Suffice to say she wouldn't be in a hurry to do it again.

Daniel wavered in a manner that would get him killed on the front line of a battlefield. As she sat down, switched on the television and started jumping between channels he ground his teeth together. But what difference did it make how long he had nightmares? Wasn't as if she could figure out the rest without help, even if she'd worked out why he moved apartments a tad too quick for his liking. Drawing a breath, he decided he could give her the one thing she wanted to know. But it was a case of give a little to get a little. Once he had answered, she was telling him what had been bothering her.

Tossing his jacket back on the chair as she settled on a channel, he walked around the sofa and sat down beside her.

'Eight years.' He eased the remote from her hand. 'And we're not watching a chick-flick.'

'We're not watching something with explosions and a high body count either,' she retorted.

'Car chases.'

'No.'

He continued scrolling through the options at the bottom of the screen. 'Alien invasion: that one's good.'

'*Nerd.*'

'Bank robbery it is, then.'

She sighed heavily. 'You're going to criticize the police procedure the whole way through this, aren't you?'

'Yup.' Tossing the remote out of her reach, he leaned back and stretched his arms over his head, casually dropping one of them on her shoulders on the way back down.

Her head turned, brows lifted as she looked into his eyes. 'Seriously?'

'What?'

'That move went out with drive-ins.'

'I heard they were making a comeback.' Setting his feet on the chest she used as a coffee table, he pulled her closer to his side.

It took another five minutes for her to take her shoes off. Tossing cushions out of the way, she leaned into him and curled her legs beside her body. Finally she took a breath and looked up at him, her voice low and soft. 'You can't have gone that long without sleep. You wouldn't be upright.'

'Eventually your body says enough's enough. I'm due an eight-hour coma soon.' He reached out and tucked a strand of hair behind her ear. 'With any luck it'll get here at night so I don't wake you up.'

She grimaced. 'Despite what you think I didn't say that to make you feel guilty.'

'I know.' But since he'd already given her more than he planned, it was his turn. 'Tell me what's been bothering you since I got here.'

Turning her head, she dropped it back against

his arm, closed her eyes and scrunched up her face. There was a low, strangled sound from the base of her throat before her eyes popped open. Then she turned towards him, tucking her legs underneath her. 'Can we talk about the whole thoughtful and protective combo you've been using on me first?'

'Okay,' he replied with suspicion.

'Could you stop doing it?'

He stifled a smile. 'Taking the independence thing a tad too far, don't you think?'

'See?' She scowled. 'You're doing it again. It's the tone you use.'

'I only have the one voice.'

'No, you don't. It changes.' Lifting a hand, she counted them off on her unfurling fingers. 'There's your considerate voice, your seductive voice, your "I'm in trouble if I don't shut up soon" voice—'

He captured her hand. 'Let's go back to the problem you have with thoughtful and protective.'

'I don't like it.'

Yes, he got that from the number of times she'd resisted it. 'Protect is what I do,' he reasoned. 'Along with the word serve it's written in big letters along the sides of vehicles with big flashing lights on top. You may have noticed them in the city.' A corner of his mouth tugged wryly as he admitted, 'Thoughtful I have to work on from time to time.'

'No,' she said with a small pout. 'You're pretty good at that one too.'

He took a breath. 'Let me get this straight. You want me to not care what happens to you and be more inconsiderate.'

Jo opened her mouth, closed it and rolled her eyes. 'It sounds stupid when you put it like that.'

'Little bit.' He nodded.

She jumped from one subject to another. 'You can't text me when I'm in work.'

'If you were busy you wouldn't have answered.'

'That's not the point. Some of those messages were…' She rocked her head from side to side while seeking a word in the air beside his head.

'I could point out it takes two people to have text sex.'

'We weren't having text sex.'

'Text foreplay,' he corrected. 'Still takes two people.'

She changed subject again. 'What happened yesterday?'

'Might need you to narrow that one down…'

'You backed off,' she said with a note of accusation.

'Said I would, didn't I?'

'Not to the point where finding food was as urgent as someone lying across the bar with a gunshot wound.'

The second he realized he'd stepped into an ambush Daniel swore viciously inside his head. He'd been right to think she knew there was something wrong. On the way home he'd put her uncharacteristic silence down to exhaustion. But she'd been thinking about it the whole time, hadn't she?

'And there's that look again.' She aimed a brief glare at him. 'I swear you're turning me into a harridan.'

'A what?'

'Never mind.'

Without warning she changed position, freeing her fingers so she could brace her hands on his shoulders as she straddled his lap. When she wriggled her hips Daniel clamped his hands on her waist to hold her still before their bodies aligned. It was difficult enough to stay one step ahead of her without the kind of moves he'd pictured them doing naked.

'Talk to me,' she demanded.

'You know I can move you off me if I want to end this conversation.' He set his feet on the floor in preparation.

'Still sitting here, aren't you?' She arched a brow. 'Did you feel bad about trying to play me?'

What the—? Daniel frowned. 'When did I do *that*?'

'All those thoughtful things you claim you have to work at—they're part of your campaign to get me into bed.'

'Considering my many skills in the art of seduction, I'm a little insulted by that.' He shook his head. 'Guy can't make the effort to be nice to you, can he?'

'Being nice isn't supposed to take effort.'

'That's the thing with resistance. It makes everything more difficult.'

'So stop resisting and tell me what happened yesterday.'

Daniel sought a safe route through the minefield they were entering and—since it seemed pointless trying—dumped pretence in favour of a little dose of honesty. 'Think you'll find it any easier to talk to me about why you still have doubts than I'm finding this?'

'No,' she admitted in a thicker voice. 'But while we're on the subject, why don't you have doubts?'

'When it comes to sleeping with you, I thought I'd made it clear where I stand.' One of his hands slipped from her waist to her hip. 'I can run through it again if you like…'

Her eyes darkened. 'Not necessary.'

'Well, then…' Sliding his hand further down her leg, he edged his fingertips beneath the hem of her skirt. Gaze fixed on her face, he watched her reaction as he touched the soft skin on the outside of her thigh.

Full lips parted as she sucked in a low breath. Her long lashes lowered as she focused on his mouth. Distracting them from the topic of conversation wouldn't take much, but while Daniel knew he could get lost in her, he sensed a small corner of her mind wouldn't be there. Selfishly he wanted it to be; for her to share with him the moments when everything became sharper, clearer, there was one common goal and nothing else mattered. No yesterday, no tomorrow, no half an hour ago or two hours from then. He wanted her to see the side of him few people did outside his working environment—before the mistakes were made or the self-recrimination could set in.

'Do you think about when this is over?' she asked in a smaller voice as if she stepped inside his thoughts. 'About the mess we could leave behind?'

'Yes,' he said roughly.

'Me too,' she whispered before distracting him with a swipe of her tongue across her lips. 'Best-case scenario, we end up in a better place than we were before. Worst case—'

'We end up saying things to each other we can never take back,' he finished.

'Yes.'

When Daniel looked into her eyes again he found enough vulnerability to punch a hole in his chest. She didn't just have doubts, she was genuinely terrified...of *him*? What had he done to frighten fearless Jo? When the thought entered his mind, he dismissed it as swiftly as it arrived. A woman didn't kiss as she did, move as she did or look at a man the way she did when she wanted him if she didn't have an intimate knowledge of sex. So what else could it be?

He thought out loud. 'Maybe the problem we have right now is trust...'

Her gaze lowered to the hands that had moved

from his shoulders to his chest. 'You're saying
you don't trust me.'

'No, babe, that's not what I'm saying.' He took
a long breath and chose his words carefully. 'I
can't promise you this won't be a mess when it's
over...'

'I know.' She smiled the same tremulous smile
that had sent up a warning flare for him in the
first place.

'Do you know I would never willingly do anything to hurt you?' It floored him how much he
needed her to know that. But even as he said the
words he knew he had to amend them. 'If anything I said or did in the past—'

'*Don't.*' She pressed a forefinger to his mouth
for a second. 'I get it. You think *I* don't trust *you.*'

'Why would you? I haven't done anything to
earn it.'

She thought it over for a second. 'It's not that I
don't trust you. I'm just—'

'Wary,' he supplied, feeling the something he
still didn't recognize expand inside his chest when
her eyes warmed at the understanding.

'Yes.'

'I'm not sure you should trust me, Jo,' he heard

his voice say. 'When I'm around you, *I* don't trust me.'

'Why not?' She used the hand on his jaw to turn his head when he broke eye contact. 'No, I need to look into your eyes when you tell me so I can see if they're there.'

'See if what's there?'

'The blue goes cloudy. You have shadows.' Her fingertips whispered over his jaw. 'They're how I know there's something you're not telling me.'

Daniel felt as if something heavy were pressing down on his chest, each breath requiring considerably more effort.

As if she could sense it, Jo angled her head and looked deeper into his eyes, her hand turning so the backs of lightly bent fingers could skim the side of his neck. 'Tell me why you don't trust yourself around me.'

'I carry a lot of baggage. I'm not willing to offload it on you.' He frowned, both at the confession and the roughness of his voice. So much for the techniques the Marines taught in the event of capture and interrogation. She might as well hand him a pen and paper so he could save them both time by mapping out the weaknesses in his lines of defence.

'You think you're the only one with baggage?'

'No.'

Hand turning, she ran her fingertips under the curved neckline of his sweater, her gaze lowering to watch what she was doing. 'Shall I tell you a secret?' she whispered as her gaze tangled with his again.

Daniel nodded, mesmerized by her eyes and hypnotized by her touch.

'I want you more than I've ever wanted anyone.' When she smiled, it was steeped in sensuality. 'I fantasize about you, what we'll be like together and how it will feel. Right now, when we're like this, I doubt my doubts.'

If she was saying what he thought she was saying…

Leaning in, she pressed her lips to the throbbing pulse on his neck. A jolt of heat seared through his body, settling hot and heavy in his groin. Moving his hands to the curve of her spine, he slid her forward on his lap, aligning their bodies the way nature intended. She took a shuddering breath when she discovered what she was doing to him, moved her hips in a way that made him stifle a groan. He wanted her with a desperation he'd never experienced before. It suddenly felt as if she were a lifeline and if he didn't grab hold of it and hold on tight—

When she whispered in his ear, her warm breath caressed his skin. 'What scares me is how I feel when I can hear you on the other side of the wall and I can't get to you. The times when you're so far away from me it feels like I can't reach out and touch you...'

Daniel had experienced similar scenarios, so he knew how it felt from her point of view. But he had never been on the other side.

She took another shuddering breath. 'I need to know that you're with me and we're in this together...'

For the first time in his life he knew what it felt like to be trapped and helpless. The kind of faith it took to hand over control. He didn't consider himself a hero when he went to work. He was just a guy doing his job, failing more often than he would prefer. The real heroes were people who trusted completely and laid their lives in another person's hands.

'I'm right here, Danny. Let go...'

The words were so low they were almost lost in the storm he could feel raging inside him. It was possible she might not have said them, the need coming more from him than from her. But even if he hadn't imagined them he couldn't let go. If he did a mountain of torn and bleeding emotions would collapse and he would be crushed under their weight. He was too worn down, too exhausted from fighting the demons who took him to hell night after night. If she knew how inadequate he was, the number of times he'd failed someone who reached out to him…

'Jo—' He choked on her name.

'Shh…' Pressing soft lips to his mouth, she fed him kiss after desperately needed kiss.

At first there was only the taste of her, her heat and a sense of glory he had never known could be found in surrender. Then she rocked her hips, grinding her heat against the tight fit of his jeans and lust exploded inside his body with the force of a percussive blast.

With the equivalent of a dying breath, Daniel dragged his mouth from hers to rasp, 'Tell me to go.'

'No.' Full lips curved into a decadent smile against his mouth. 'Make love to me, Danny. *Take me to bed.*'

It was the sweetest command he'd ever been given.

CHAPTER TEN

'Mix and match can have a disastrous outcome if you get it wrong. But step outside your comfort zone and you might discover something unique.'

DENSE lashes fluttered as he started to wake up, the movement absurdly delicate against the masculinity of his face.

Jo smiled when she was looking into vivid blue eyes. 'Good morning, sleepyhead.'

''Morning,' his deep voice replied, the mattress dipping as he rolled towards her. 'What time is it?'

'Saturday o'clock and I believe your shift doesn't start until midnight.' Moving closer to the edge of the pillow, she rested her cheek on her palm. 'I've been thinking...'

'Uh-oh...'

'You know what I've never done?'

'Spent the night waking someone up so you can sleep?'

It was the kind of opening she could have used to get him to talk to her. But considering the major step forward they'd taken in intimacy she found herself wary of taking an equally giant step back. 'I've never spent the day in bed with a sexy naked guy,' she confessed with a dramatic sigh. 'Don't suppose you know where I could find one?'

'I prefer not to start my day with hitting some-one.'

'Guess I'll have to settle for you, then.'

He smiled lazily. 'How come?'

'Because you're the only naked guy here?'

'I meant how come you've never spent a day in bed with a sexy naked guy before?'

'Workaholic.' She rolled her eyes. 'Sad, I know.'

'No,' he said in a lower voice. 'Just surprising…'

'There's a little more to my job than sitting in a coffee shop three times a week.'

'After seeing your work schedule I don't doubt that.' He stretched his large body, claiming even more of the bed. 'What I find tough to believe is some other guy hasn't *tried*.'

Jo stifled another smile. 'Correct me if I'm wrong, but until recently weren't you convinced men were throwing me out of their apartments in the middle of the night?'

'That was before I knew you better.'

'And you think you know me better now?'

'I'd like to hope so.' He took a long breath. 'But it's more a case of show than tell.'

Heat flared through her body when he slanted his mouth over hers. Her skin was hyper-sensitive, as if everywhere he'd kissed and caressed while he undressed her had been branded by his touch. If there had been any question her body was tuned into his there was no doubt now. His need magnified hers. His desire for her made her want him more. For years they had been unable to hold a conversation but in one night it felt as if they'd learnt to communicate without words. He dragged his mouth from her lips to blaze a heated trail down her neck, his magic fingers skimming her body from hip to waist. A purr of sinful pleasure ran through her body in response; the combination of strong male and gentle touch unbelievably carnal. But when he moved his hand higher and got to her ribs, she squirmed.

'Mmm,' he hummed in a low, vibrating rumble into her ear. 'That I didn't know.'

'Don't,' she warned unconvincingly.

He did it again.

Amid squeaks of protest and bursts of laughter,

naked limbs tangled with sheets. Deeper chuckles of laughter joined hers, filling her with a sudden burst of undiluted joy. When they rolled off the edge of the bed and she landed on top of him, Jo leaned back and blew a strand of hair out of her eyes. She still didn't know why their relationship had changed, but as she smiled down at his grinning face it didn't matter.

All that mattered was he looked as happy as she felt.

Beyond happiness she could feel an irresistible, heart-warming tenderness. Whether it came from him or from her, she didn't know. She ran her fingertips over early morning shadow and warm skin, her gaze studying the different shades of blue in his amazing eyes. How he had looked at her as their bodies joined together was something she would never forget. It felt as if he had given her something she never had to give back. To deny she had given him something in return was pointless.

For the first time, instead of allowing someone to occupy a tiny corner of her heart, she'd given part of it away.

Without warning emotion clogged her throat. Leaving him would be one of the most difficult things she'd ever had to do. How was she supposed to tell him she was leaving when she couldn't cushion it with the confession she didn't want to go? She would miss him. But she'd been alone before. She could do it again. She didn't have a choice. Not if giving up the dream within her grasp meant replacing it with one she could never—

'What is it?' he asked in a deeper, rougher voice.

Unwilling to take a chance he would know she was lying—even if it was just with a shake of her head—she leaned down and pressed her mouth to his. The one more minute she'd once wanted had become one more day. She didn't want what they had to be over yet. She wasn't ready to let go.

In the absence of honesty, she sought the lightness she'd been aiming for when he awoke.

'Know what else I figured out when I was thinking?' she mumbled against his lips. 'A woman must have taught you some of those moves you used on me last night.'

'Not going there,' he mumbled back.

'I'm thinking older woman, younger Danny...'

His mouth curled into a smile. 'Jealous?'

'Since I'm reaping the benefits I was thinking more along the lines of a thank-you card...'

'What makes you think I'm not a natural or inspired?'

'Inspired is good. I'd roll with that if I were you.'

He did, reaching a hand above them for a pillow when Jo was pinned beneath him. Tucking it beneath her head, he smiled a predatory smile. 'This whole day in bed—does it have to be *in* the bed to count?'

She batted her lashes. 'What did you have in mind?'

'Again,' he said in a rumble so soft it was more like a vibration in his chest. 'More a case of show than tell...'

The 'interrupt the interrupted sleep' ploy was clever; he had to give her that. He was feeling better than he had in...

Yeah, it had been a while.

The first real test of how well they were doing appeared on their third night together. When he jolted into reality she was staring at him with wide, fear-filled eyes. But it hadn't been fear for herself, it was fear for *him*. Daniel felt the whispered caress of her touch soothing him. But when he looked at his hands and saw how tight he was holding her upper arms, he was filled with horror.

What the hell was he doing? A wave of nausea rolled over him at the thought of leaving a bruise on her skin and he knew he had to get away from her. *Fast.*

She hadn't tried to stop him when he said he was going to run it out of his system. But before he left, her soft voice asked, 'What did it mean?'

He froze in the doorway. 'What did what mean?'

'You kept saying you needed two more; two of what?'

He walked away without answering. But despite the vow he made to place some distance between them, after a quiet shift filled with thoughts of her he was back at her door. Seeing her robbed him of his ability to speak. Determined to show her how much he needed her when unable to say it aloud, he kissed her welcoming smile and took her straight back to bed. One eight hour coma later and he was able to demonstrate what a damn fine specimen of manhood he could be when firing on all six cylinders. Unfortunately, it also meant something else.

But if he was being forced to leave her bed again he was determined to give her an afternoon to remember.

Leaning against a tree at the edge of the photo-shoot in Central Park, his gaze took in the details of a world he knew next to nothing about. Judging from what he had observed he wouldn't have the patience, whereas Jo seemed to thrive on it. She was animated, lively and enthusiastic; sparkling as if she inhabited some kind of secret magical kingdom. She obviously loved what she did. It glowed from her eyes.

For a second he found himself curious what it would feel like to have her look at *him* that way. But since it made the something he didn't want to identify ache in his chest...

'And that's a wrap, boys and girls!'

While models and assistants breathed a visible sigh of relief, the photographer held out a hand to Jo and waggled his fingers. 'Hand it over, my sweet. Have to be careful what awful images of me you place in the public domain...'

'With someone as photogenic as you?' Jo scoffed as she gave him a small digital camera.

Head bowed, he scrolled through the images. 'Not that one. *Definitely* not that one, and when I've deleted everything which doesn't meet my approval we can discuss your new friend.'

'What new friend?'

'The guy who has been watching your every

move for the last fifteen minutes.' Waving a hand at a security guard with a silent let him through as Jo's gaze found Daniel, he made the comment, 'Obviously doesn't work in fashion...'

'No,' she replied. 'He's a—'

'Don't tell me. It's much more fun to fantasize.'

Daniel stepped over the line to claim his place beside her. 'Hey, babe.'

'Hello, handsome.' The photographer grinned.

Jo bit her lip and stifled a chuckle. '*Behave.* Christophe Devereaux, Daniel Brannigan. Danny, this is Chris.'

'Explains a lot about the smile you've been wearing this morning,' the man remarked as he looked Daniel over. 'How long have you been dating? Because seriously, honey, those clothes?'

'Kinda work for him, don't you think?'

'I suppose, in a blue collar kind of way. But picture him in Armani or Gucci or maybe a little—'

'Not gonna happen,' Daniel said dryly when he got tired of being talked about as if he weren't there. Being objectified was both uncomfortable and unfamiliar and since he'd been dressing himself from the age of two, he didn't need any help.

'Not a fan of labels,' Jo felt the need to explain.

It wasn't necessary in Daniel's opinion. He didn't have to answer to anyone, least of all a guy who obviously spent too much time in front of a mirror.

Christophe blinked. 'Well, *that* must be refreshing…'

Judging by the soft, almost affectionate smile she gave him, Daniel assumed it was a good thing. Somewhat pathetically it forced him to resist the urge to smirk at her friend. Five minutes in her magical kingdom and he suspected he wouldn't be viewed as much of a prince.

'You done for the day?' he asked.

'Yes. But you already knew that or you wouldn't be here. *Someone* obviously sneaked a look at my planner this morning…' Leaning forward, she placed the air kisses Daniel had always hated above each of her friend's cheeks. 'I owe you one for today. Thanks for letting me sit in.'

'We'll call it even for the support you gave me when I was a virtual unknown; nothing quite like a mention on that blog of yours to raise one's profile.' He aimed a haughty, almost territorial look at Daniel. 'Take care of her or you'll have me to deal with.'

Somehow managing to keep a straight face,

Daniel gave him a nod in reply. It wasn't much of a threat. What was the guy going to do, fluff him to death? Eager to leave, he took Jo's hand. 'Let's go.'

'Just out of curiosity,' she said as they walked through the park, 'what would you have done if I'd met Liv today the way I was supposed to?'

'Still bugging you, isn't it?'

'That I'm keeping something from my best friend?'

'Even when we come out there will be certain things you can't discuss with her, you know that, right?'

Her eyes widened. '*When* we come out?'

Oh, no, she didn't. 'We're not arguing today. I have plans for what's left of it.'

'Where are we going?'

'Wait and see.'

'Is it a surprise?' She brightened. 'For *me*?'

He smiled when it literally put a skip in her step. 'Do I need to explain the concept of wait and see?'

'Are we there yet?'

'No.'

Several repetitions of the same Q&A later, he stopped in the middle of a path and her brows lifted in anticipation.

'You have two choices. Zoo—' he jerked a thumb over his shoulder '—or that...'

Leaning to the side to look around him, she stilled and for a moment Daniel thought he'd got it wrong. Then her face lit up. 'Are you kidding me?' She threw herself at him. 'I *love* this!' After a tight hug, she stepped back and grasped hold of his hands. 'You're coming on all the rides, right?'

'I'm not sitting on the little wooden horses.'

'Ever kiss a girl on a carousel?'

'Wouldn't that be kissing and telling?'

As they stepped through the gates she turned towards him. 'I refuse to participate in my surprise until you agree to do everything with me.' She focused on his mouth, looked into his eyes and smiled meaningfully. 'But I promise to make it worth your while if you do...'

'Attempting to bribe a police officer?' Daniel assumed a deadpan expression. 'You know I can arrest you for that.'

'*Silly.*' She rolled her eyes. 'If you put me in a cell for the night how will you collect your reward?'

If he was getting to spend the night with her it would be a good point. 'You want pink fluffy stuff on a stick or do you want to eat something sensible?'

'Pink and fluffy.' She tugged on his hand. 'We can take it on the carousel with us.'

Leaning against a ridiculous-looking wooden horse was as much of a compromise as he was prepared to make. While the platform began to move he watched her suck her fingers before peeling off another lump of fluffy candy. She'd been driving him crazy with that move while they stood in line; the glint in her eyes telling him she knew exactly what she was doing. Reaching out, he curled his hand around the back of her neck and pressed his mouth to hers. Intended as punishment for her actions, it instead led to the first sugar rush of his life. When he lifted his head she stayed where she was, eyes closed and a blissful smile on her face.

She sighed. 'Carousels officially rock my world.'

Daniel smiled. Not as much as she rocked his.

Several rides later, he was hooked on her enjoyment and feeling pretty damn proud of himself for satisfying her need for fun. It was another thing he could add to his new list, having scrapped the one he made before they got involved. Now she was his to take care of, his to protect and her needs were his to satisfy; the mantra of *his, his, his* going a long way towards pacifying his inner Neanderthal every time one of the guys running a ride was foolish enough to flirt with her.

They took a break to grab a couple of soft pretzels with mustard. Jo shared her pretzel with a horde of cocky, well-fed pigeons while Daniel managed to share a dollop of mustard with his jeans. Biting down on a corner of her lower lip when he did it, she helpfully tried to remove the stain with a paper napkin until he was forced to remind her they were in a public place. Where there were *children* present. After a leisurely kiss to promise she could do whatever she wanted to him when they got home he watched as she looked over the crowd and smiled. Following her line of vision he discovered one of the children he'd mentioned with what was either a mother or a nanny; lightning-fast fingers fixing a braid in dark hair.

'Do you remember her?' he asked.

'My mom?'

When her smile faded a little, Daniel sought out a hint of regret for asking but couldn't find it. Hypocritical as it was, he wanted to know everything about her while remaining unable to give her the same in return.

He nodded. 'Yeah.'

Jo took a short breath and thought about what to tell him the way she always did when they discussed a subject she found difficult. It was how he knew when she was sharing things with him she hadn't told anyone else, the knowledge both humbling and adding to his guilt for being unable to do the same.

'Little things,' she replied as she fed the last of her pretzel to the pigeons. 'I can remember how she brushed my hair. She used to follow the brush with her hand.' A hint of wistful smile appeared. 'I still do that.'

'I know.' It was part of her morning routine. Watching her dress was almost as fascinating to him as taking her clothes off. When she looked at him in a way that suggested she knew what he was thinking he added another prompt. 'Keep going.'

There was another moment of thought as she selected a gift for him from a cache of precious memories. 'She used to hum when she was doing housework. My dad would say one of the reasons he loved her was because she had a song in her heart. He used to wink at me before he sneaked up behind her to dance with her. It drove her crazy if she was in the middle of doing something but she always laughed.' Jo nodded and smiled again. 'She had a great laugh.'

'What did she look like?'

'On rare occasions Jack will tell me how much I look like her.' She shrugged, the smile disappearing as she hid the hint of pain in her eyes with a blink of long lashes. 'I think it made it difficult for him to look at me when she was gone.'

Despite the matter-of-fact tone to her voice it was the first time he'd felt any empathy for her father. Daniel didn't want to imagine a world without Jo in it but he knew it would be a darker place. 'When did you start calling him Jack?'

'When he stopped being my dad.' She looked into his eyes and angled her chin. 'What was your dad like?'

Swift change of subject noted, Daniel shook his head and avoided her gaze. 'You already know the answer to that.'

'I know what everyone else in your family remembers.'

'You'd be better sticking with their impression. They argued with him less.'

'What did you argue about?'

'His disappointment in me was a favourite topic.'

Disbelief sounded in her voice. 'He *said* that?'

'With due cause.' He glanced at her from the corner of his eye, unwilling to go into detail beyond, 'None of the others ever mention how close I was to being the first Brannigan on the wrong side of the law?'

Her eyes widened. *'Shut up.'*

Pushing to his feet, Daniel turned and held out a hand, drawing her upright when her palm slipped into his. 'What do you want to do next?'

She smiled brightly. 'Finish talking about this comes to mind. I want to know what kind of trouble you got into.'

'And take a chance you might look at me differently?' A frown crossed his face as they walked towards a line of stalls. It was closer to the truth than he cared to admit. But since he wasn't convinced he wanted to know why, he left it alone.

'Well, *that* deserves a suitable punishment,' she retorted. When he glanced at her again, she was looking around. Her eyes lit up. 'Marines can hit targets, right?'

An hour later, he was trying to figure out how he'd ended up being the one carrying a three foot stuffed rabbit through the park. If making him feel like an idiot had been her goal he wasn't the only one who could hit a target. He held it up by long ears and gazed at it in disgust. 'It's cross-eyed.'

'Our imperfections make us unique,' her voice replied from above his head. 'Didn't anyone ever tell you that?'

Daniel looked at the pond. 'I wonder if it floats.'

'You *wouldn't.*'

'You can go get it when you fall off those rocks.'

'You see…' She turned and cocked a hip. 'I heard from a reliable source it's all about balance…'

He shook his head when she had to hold her arms out to her sides to stay upright. 'I'm not wading in after you.'

'You've got a lot to learn about when a girl wants to be rescued and when she doesn't.' She turned her back to him and held her arms above her head. *'Catch.'*

Taking an immediate step forward when he realized what she was doing, he caught her in his arms as she fell.

'And you didn't drop the bunny either.' She grinned after checking. *'My hero.'*

Daniel nodded. 'You can use it as a life-preserver.'

Stepping closer to the edge of the water and swinging her back and forth, he smiled when she protested between bouts of lyrical laughter. Stilling, he looked down at her, his gaze roving over her face as he found himself wondering why it had taken so long to open his eyes and see what was right in front of him. Would it have made a difference if they'd got together earlier? Would his life go back to the way it was before when they were done? Maybe he should try to talk to her about—

'That one's new,' she murmured.

'What is?'

'The look in your eyes…'

Before he could scramble his way out of it or distract her with a kiss there was the sound of tinkling music.

She sighed heavily. 'That's my cell phone.'

'Don't answer it.'

'I have to.' She wriggled in his arms until he set her on her feet. Predictably the call resulted in the disappearance of Jo and the reappearance of dull, emotionless Jo.

Before she could say the usual words at the end

of the phone call, he took a breath and held out his arm. 'I'm not carrying this thing on the subway.'

'A gentleman would,' she pointed out.

'Pity you're dating me, then, isn't it?'

She didn't try to stop him coming with her. But she would if she knew what he was planning to do. He'd had enough. First opportunity he got— and he would damn well *make one*—Daniel was having that talk with Jack. Way he saw it, it was overdue.

CHAPTER ELEVEN

'When shopping it's important to keep an open mind. You can't always get what you want but be patient and you might discover exactly what you need.'

'I BETTER make him something to eat,' she said when they got Jack to his apartment a little after dark.

Daniel nodded. 'What else?'

'Check he has groceries.'

'You get what he needs from the store across the street. I'll make him something to eat.' When she wavered he added a firm, '*Go*. I've got this.'

Ignoring the voice in her head, Jo reached for her purse. If she was totally honest, breaking the habit of a lifetime to accept help probably stemmed from the need for a little space. As much as she had loved their afternoon together and felt bad for once again having to interrupt it, the one day she wanted kept turning into another and another. But she couldn't keep stealing memories, threading them together like glowing beads on a precious necklace. She had to tell him, especially when hiding it was slowly killing her. Trouble was she still didn't know why it was so darn difficult to find the words.

Seemed to Jo she'd been spilling her guts on pretty much every other subject, including things she'd never shared with anyone else. He was almost as good at getting her to do that as he was at avoiding sharing anything with her that did more than scratch the surface of his life.

Yes, that was bugging her too.

Halfway to the store she realized she hadn't checked the refrigerator to see what was there. But when she returned to the apartment she heard Daniel's voice say, 'I think it's time we had a talk.'

Jo froze inside the doorway. What was he doing?

'I'm only gonna say this once. You might not care what effect your actions have on your daughter, but I do. Cause her any heartache I'll be in your face 24/7. We clear?'

She was about to take a step forward when Jack replied, 'I love my Jo.'

'Did you love her when she ended up living on the streets because of you?' Daniel asked bluntly.

'She could have died. Someone she knew did—she tell you that?'

'No.'

'Course she didn't. Jo deals with things on her own; kills her to ask for help even with small stuff. If she knew I was talking to you right now she would kick my ass.'

True. Or at least be angry with him for interfering. But instead she remained frozen to the spot, unable to breathe.

'She's like her mom,' Jack said.

'Losing her that way can't have been easy.'

'It wasn't.'

'I'm sorry, Jack,' Daniel said with sincerity. 'I genuinely am. But do you think your wife would be happy Jo lost both her parents that day?'

Jo's eyes widened. How did he know that?

'If you want to honour her memory, this isn't the way to do it.' Daniel's voice took on the rough edge that always got to her. 'One day your beautiful daughter will meet someone, get married and have kids of her own. You want to miss out on your grandkids too? Wouldn't your wife want you to look for a piece of both of you in their eyes?'

Jack cleared his throat and answered, 'She would.'

The pain in his voice made Jo regret all the times they hadn't talked about her mom. They should have. But at eight she had found grief hard to handle and in later years she'd had too many other things to deal with. Then it was too late. Or so she'd thought. Hadn't been when she talked to Daniel, had it? Memories of her mom had flowed off her tongue as if they'd needed to be said. There had to be trust between them for her to have done that. The same trust that allowed her to stand silently by a door and let Daniel handle Jack his way.

She'd never let anyone do that before.

'You're going to have to shape up,' Daniel said. 'If I was the father of those kids I don't think I could trust you with them. But I'd want them to get to know you in the same way I'd want them to know about their grandmother. It would be nice if they could hear it from the man who loved her.'

Jo looked down and realized she had set a palm on her stomach. There was no question of her being pregnant but she had never thought about the kind of man she would want to be the father of her children. Frankly she'd never thought about *having* children. After all, she was twenty-four, wasn't like there was a rush. But with his mile-wide protective streak she knew Daniel would be an amazing dad. The thought of smaller versions of him another woman had given him...

Wow. Jo really didn't like that image *at all*.

'Still love her,' Jack said in a low voice.

'You ever think about getting grief counselling? I know someone who runs a group. It won't stop you drinking—you're the only one who can do that—but it might do you good to talk about her.' There was a brief pause before Daniel said, 'Lock stuff away, it can be harder to deal with. Trust me, I *know*.'

'You're a good man,' Jack said. 'Glad my girl has you in her life.'

So was she. There were dozens of things she would never forget about her time with him. But suddenly it didn't feel like enough any more.

'I'll drop the card by next week,' Daniel's voice said. 'Now let's see what we can get done before Jo comes back.'

As they moved she slipped back through the door, quietly closing it behind her. At the bottom of the stairs she swiped her cheeks and stared at the moisture she found on her hands. Crying was right up there with blushing on the list of things she never did. What was happening to her?

Pushing through the door, she walked across the street in a daze. She felt as if she was in shock. Not the least little bit as she'd thought she would feel if she fell in love. Surely feeling so numb meant she *wasn't* in love? Inside the store she picked up a basket and wandered aimlessly along the aisle. If she hadn't known there was a chance she was *falling* in love then what had she been so afraid of? Why was it so difficult to tell him she was leaving? Would she have reacted the way she did to the image of kids she hadn't given him?

Was she having a teensy little bit of a meltdown?

If it hadn't felt that way she might have reacted quicker when she rounded the corner. But by the time she realized what was happening it was too late.

Where was she?

With everything squared away and Jack sound asleep on the covers of his rack, Daniel drummed his fingers on the kitchen counter. He checked his wristwatch. She should have been back already. Restless, he decided to go look for her.

Jogging down the stairs and across the street, he opened the door to the convenience store and checked the aisles. No Jo. Walking to where he

assumed the checkout was he rounded a corner.
There she was. An unwarranted sense of relief
washed over him, but when her gaze darted to
him and a brief look of agony crossed her face,
he knew something was wrong.

Stilling, he looked to his left. *Son of a—*

'Don't move!'

Swiftly identifying the weapon pointed at the
man behind the counter, Daniel made eye contact with the perp holding it. 'Take it easy. No one
needs to get hurt.'

'Anyone come in with you?'

'No.' He took an instinctive step closer to Jo to
shield her body with his. 'But you might want to
think about locking the doors.'

'I said *don't move!*'

An unfamiliar buzz of fear swarmed over him,
immediately replaced by a gathering rage he
had to beat off with a mental stick. Since going
Marine on the guy who'd placed his woman in
danger wasn't going to help anyone but him,
Daniel reined in his emotions and replaced them
with rigid control. 'I'm just gonna lock that one.'

Without looking at her, he pointed a finger at the
door a couple of feet past Jo. From what he could
tell it was one of only two points of entry for a

tactical team. While placing her within snatch and grab territory, it also put her directly in the line of fire. Daniel would take a bullet before he let anything happen to her. It was as simple as that.

'Why are you helping me?' The perp's gaze shifted between each of his hostages before he came to the conclusion Daniel was the greater threat.

Good call.

'I'd prefer not to get shot.' When a low gasp came from over his shoulder as the gun swung towards him, Daniel shrugged his shoulders and sent her a hidden message. 'I've got a hot date with a fiery redhead tonight.'

She was smart enough not to mention he was a cop, but he didn't want her to identify him by name. If an association was made between them, she could be used for leverage.

'Give him the money,' he told the man behind the counter.

'I don't want money. I want *my kid*,' yelled gun guy.

Couldn't walk into a simple hold-up, could she?

'I already said she's not here,' said the man behind the counter, drawing the perp's focus.

'Then you call her and get her to bring him

down here.' The gun turned sideways, prodding the air. 'Do it *now*!'

Daniel moved his arm back and pointed his finger at the ground to indicate Jo should get behind him. In his peripheral vision he saw the slight shake of her head. She had chosen the wrong time to defy him. If he didn't have a job to do they'd be having the argument of a lifetime.

Sirens sounded in the distance.

'You called the cops?' the guy yelled.

Since he doubted the convenience store had a silent alarm, Daniel assumed a witness called 911. 'Still time to get out…'

The gun shifted direction again. 'Did *you* call them?'

'With my record?'

'What did you do?'

'Dealing.' He patted a pocket of his jacket to gauge the level of interest. 'Get us out of here before the cops arrive, I'll give you a sample.'

'I want my kid.'

So much for that idea. 'You do what you gotta do but I can't be here. They find me carrying, I violate my parole.'

'No one's going anywhere till I get my kid.'

'You've got hostages. They'll send in a SWAT

team.' Daniel suppressed a threatening smile in case it fed into his deep-seated need to go feral. 'I heard those guys shoot first, ask questions later.' When his words garnered a glance towards the back of the store, he took a step forward. 'Let's go.'

'They'll catch us.'

Another step. 'Not if we move now.'

'I need time to think.'

Another step. 'I'm not going back inside.'

'Shut up and let me think!'

When there was a low clicking that indicated a round had been chambered, Daniel knew he was out of time.

'Get down!'

Launching forward, he grasped the gun arm, pushing it back and up. Tins scattered as he slammed it against a metal shelf. Once, twice and there was a cry of pain before the gun hit the ground. He kicked it out of reach, stepped forward, hooked an ankle and toppled the guy back onto the floor. Dropping to his knee, he flipped the body over, twisting the arm he held as he reached for the other one. From the moment he moved until the guy was restrained took less than ten seconds.

Once it was done, his gaze immediately sliced through the air to Jo. 'You okay?'

She nodded.

It didn't slow his heart rate. If anything, the fact she was standing on her feet added to the flood of rage he'd been suppressing. Which part of *'get down'* hadn't she got?

'I'm okay,' another voice announced, making Daniel swear viciously inside his head. There had been two hostages, Officer Brannigan, count them; one, *two.*

'Both of you get out of here. *Now.*' As he fought the red haze rapidly forming around the edge of his vision, he turned his head and saw her take a step towards him. 'I mean it, Jo,' he warned. 'You walk out that door, you go straight to the nearest squad car and you damn well stay there.'

It was the first time since his pre-Marine days he'd been angry enough to yell his damn head off. He'd let her leave the apartment alone. Better still, he'd *sent her* to the store. If he hadn't gone looking for her, if he hadn't been there, if a loose round had gone off...

Grinding his teeth together, he focused on deep, measured breaths. His initial reaction was they'd gone beyond a promise she'd never go to the neighbourhood alone at night. If he had his way she'd be lucky to ever see daylight again. His second thought was every day of a life they shared would be a battle between her independence and his need to protect her. Fact was she didn't belong in his world any more than he did in hers.

'Who *are* you?' asked a muffled voice from the floor.

'You don't stay still, I'll be your ticket to the nearest emergency room.' Adjusting his position, he reached into the back pocket of his jeans. When he heard footsteps, he held his badge over his head.

'Yeah, we know. Still got a bit of a problem with taking time off, don't you?'

He glanced upwards. 'Hey, Dom.'

'Hey, Danny.' Dom grinned.

As the perp was cuffed and taken from him, Daniel got to his feet and headed for the door. He'd known the payback for his eight-hour coma was going to be a bitch, been prepared to pay the price when he knew there was time with Jo as a reward for holding on to his sanity. But to have one of the scenarios associated with his nightmares become *reality*...

As he crossed the street his gaze cut through

flashing lights to locate her. Adrenalin still pump-
ing, every tense muscle in his body strained with
the need to get to her, haul her into his arms and
never let go. But as she started to turn towards
him, he stopped dead in his tracks.

For a second everything simply went silent.

Then it hit him.

How could he not have known? How in hell had
he not seen it coming? He'd stood on the edge of
bridges, rappelled out of choppers, faced gun-
fire, crawled into narrow spaces where he could
be crushed like a bug and had never once been
as fearful as he was in that store. And now he
knew why.

Turning away before she looked at him, Daniel
dug out his cell phone. The call he made for back-
up would most likely add to the fallout but he
needed time to regroup and he couldn't do that
when she was there.

Unable to tear her gaze from him for long, Jo
watched as he paced the street while talking on
the phone. She wanted to be strong. As calm and
collected as he was. But in comparison to the
numbness she felt walking into the store, her emotions were all over the place. If he'd been shot…
if she'd *lost* him while he tried to protect her…

'You're Danger Danny's girl?'

Nodding, she dragged her gaze from him to look at the uniformed officer. 'I'm Jo.'

'Dom Molloy—I worked with Danny out of the ninth before he moved to the ESU. It's nice to meet you, Jo.' The dark-haired man smiled in greeting. 'I need to ask some questions and take a statement. You feel up to that?'

She nodded again. 'Yes.'

'We'll go over here where it's quieter.'

'Okay.' Jo looked over her shoulder at Daniel while they left. She didn't want to be somewhere she couldn't see him, but she wasn't going to let him down. She would answer all of the questions clearly and concisely and make sure everyone knew how amazing he had been. The need to step into his arms and stay there until some of his warmth and strength seeped into her shaking body would have to wait.

In comparison to the event itself, which had happened in slow motion, the wrap-up seemed to fly by. Next thing she knew a voice called her name and she was blinking in surprise.

Liv folded her in a brief, tight hug before studying her face with concern. 'Are you okay?'

'I'm fine.' Her gaze moved from Liv to Blake

and then back to Liv again. 'What are you doing here?'

'Danny called.'

'She was too wound up to drive,' Blake explained.

'What he means is I was worried sick about you.'

Jo opened her mouth to say there was no need when a deep voice sounded behind her and her breath caught.

'She's given a statement. She can go now.'

Spinning on her heels, she looked up at Daniel and drank in the sight of him. Her gaze lowered briefly to his chest to take inventory while she curled her fingers into fists at her sides. He was okay, she reassured her pounding heart. He was *right there*. She could stand and look at him without feeling the need to cling to him like a drowning woman. She *could*!

'What happened?' Liv asked.

'Suspected EDP; she walked into a 10-52.'

Jo had no idea what that meant but she was too busy trying to keep her head above an unexpected wave of pain to ask. The image was too close to her earliest memory of him—the ache to have him acknowledge her existence as desperate as it had been back then. If Mr Cool-Calm-And-Collected didn't look at her soon she was going to—

'Why are you in street clothes?' Liv inevitably asked.

'I'm off duty,' her brother replied.

'Then why are you here?'

'None of your business,' he said in his don't-mess-with-me voice. 'And if you cross-examine her on the way home there'll be one less monkey-suited brother at your wedding.'

'Like Mom will let that happen.'

Daniel crossed his jaw. 'Get her out of here, Liv.'

'Wait a minute.' When he walked away, Jo followed him. 'I don't even merit a "see you later"?'

He kept walking.

'Come back here.' She scowled at his broad back. *'Danny!'*

He turned and looked her straight in the eye. 'If I come back over there I'm going to yell at you.'

Even hidden behind a mask of restraint, the force of his anger knocked her back on her heels. She was wrong. He wasn't the least little bit cool and calm. Judging by the set of his shoulders he was barely collected. It might not have been the reaction she'd hoped for but it was better than nothing.

'What were you doing in there?' she asked in a far from steady voice.

'My job.'

'Is part of your job to see how many times you can almost get yourself killed before you get it right?'

'If it costs our life to get someone out, that's the price we pay.' He waved an arm at his side. 'Ask any of these guys in a uniform and they'll tell you the same thing.'

She gaped at him. 'You have no idea why I'm upset right now, do you?'

'I *warned you* about the danger in this neighbourhood,' he replied through gritted teeth.

'You're *blaming me* for this?' She could hear her voice rising. 'Do you think I went looking for a speeding bullet so you could jump in front of it and prove me wrong about needing to be rescued? I *know* the risks you take for other people, Danny. I just don't want you to take them *for me.*'

'I'm supposed to stand there and let you get shot?'

The thread she was hanging from snapped. 'Do you think I wanted you in there? I spent every second after I walked into that mess *praying* you wouldn't come find me! I knew what you would do but knowing and seeing it happen are two different things. Danger is *your* addiction, Danny, not mine. I know it doesn't matter to you who it is you're trying to save—'

'*It doesn't matter who—?*' He clamped his mouth shut, then nodded firmly. 'That's it. You're leaving now.'

'I'm not—' When he stepped forward, Jo took a step back. '*Don't you dare!*' He bent at the knee and tossed her over his shoulder, marching forward while she struggled. 'Put me down, Danny! I *hate* when you do this.'

'Where's your car?' he barked at his sister.

'End of the street,' she replied on what sounded like a note of amusement.

'Don't *help* him.' Jo lifted her hands, attempting to get her hair out of her eyes so she could glare at his sister. 'I want you to file for a restraining order. If you don't I'm reporting your unmitigated jackass of a brother for assault.'

He tossed her higher up his shoulder and kept walking.

Not caring if she was dropped on her rear, Jo continued fighting. 'You might have fooled me for a while, you great ape, but now I remember everything that bugged me most about you.'

He stopped and swung her from side to side before asking, 'Jeep on the corner?'

'Yes,' Blake said.

Was no one on *her* side?

'Don't for a single second think we're kissing
and making up after this either,' she said without
thinking as he started walking again. 'There isn't
anything you can say or do that—'

'Did she just say kissing?' Liv asked.

'Yup,' Blake replied.

Daniel dropped her onto her feet by the Jeep and
aimed a filthy look her way. *'Well done.'*

'Like they hadn't figured it out already,' Jo bit
back before glancing at Liv. 'Thanks for jumping
to my defence.'

'After you kept this little secret?'

'Leave her alone,' Daniel warned.

A burst of laughter left his sister's lips. 'Oh, I
haven't even got started on you yet. If you think
I'm not going to ask what your intentions are towards my best friend—'

'This is where I tend to leave them to it,' Blake
told Jo in a low voice.

'Tempting,' she replied. 'But give me a minute.'
Placing a thumb and forefinger between her lips,
she whistled loudly.

When the siblings looked at her, she drew on her rapidly waning strength and looked at Daniel first. 'You're in enough trouble already. If you weren't such an idiot you would know what I needed to avoid this meltdown when you walked out of the store. In case you hadn't got it already, protecting me from your sister *wasn't it.*' She turned her attention to Liv. 'And if you can think of a way I could have told you I was using one of your brothers to test the chocolate theory, feel free to let me know.' She glared at each of them in turn and lifted her chin. 'Anything else anyone wants to say?'

'I'm good.' Liv nodded before looking at Daniel. 'You?'

He glanced down at her from the corner of his eye. 'I ever thank you for bringing her home with you?'

'You're welcome.'

When he looked at her, Jo could feel some of his anger had dissipated, but not by much. She really didn't think she could take much more. For sixteen years she had stood on her own two feet, faced everything life threw at her and *nothing* had ever got to her the way he did. She should hate him for that, but she didn't. That was the problem. She felt so many things at once she couldn't untangle them to make sense of it all.

'Finished yelling at me now?' he asked in a gruff voice.

Oh, that was *so* unfair. He'd even managed to say it in a way that made it feel as if she weren't the only one struggling. The girl who had always considered herself a fighter had never felt the need to run away more keenly.

'You want me to leave? Congratulations, Danny, *you win*.' The secret she'd kept tripped off the tip of her tongue. 'I'm booked on a flight to Paris in six days.'

Daniel looked stunned. 'What?'

'You heard me. No big deal, right? Just moves our schedule up a little.' Unable to continue looking at him and with her throat closing over, Jo turned away. When she reached for a handle to open the Jeep, her shoulders slumped. 'Can someone open the door, please?' There was a high-pitched blip and a click of locks. 'Thank you.'

The trip home was long and interminably silent, but Jo didn't want to talk. Instead she turned her head and watched the blur of colours and lights and people as the city went by. It wasn't how she'd wanted to tell him, but it was done now and there was nothing she could do to take it back.

'Where are we going?' she asked when something outside the windows didn't seem quite right.

'Our place,' Liv replied.

Jo shook her head. 'No, Liv, I want to go home.'

They conceded without too much fuss, which Jo appreciated in her exhaustive state. But after insisting she would see her all the way into the apartment, Liv turned to her with concern in her eyes. 'You're not okay, are you?'

Jo shook her head.

'Brannigan men can be a little thick-skulled. But Danny—'

'Liv—' Jo grimaced '—please don't.'

'Just this one thing and then I'll stop.' She took a short breath. 'Back when Danny was a kid he could make his body and his hands do whatever he wanted them to do. I heard he could toss a perfect spiral with a football at two—throw a killer curve with a baseball at three. Dad thought it made him cocky; felt he had to bring him down a peg or two by pushing him till he learnt he had limits. All it did in the end was make Danny twice as determined, ten times harder on himself, and half as communicative. Dad never broke him, not on the surface. But it doesn't mean he doesn't have feelings or can't be hurt...'

'I know,' Jo said on a harsh whisper.

'Try telling him what Paris means to you and he might—'

Emotion clogged her throat again. *'Liv—'*

'I'm stopping now.' She folded Jo into another hug. 'You had a rough night. Go get some sleep. I'll check in on you in the morning.'

Jo stood in the centre of the room for a long time after her best friend left, feeling more alone than she'd ever been. Paris had been her dream for a long time. But with it far off in the distance she'd never spared a moment to think about the things she would leave behind. She had worked long and hard, fought for a sense of security and been blessed with more than she dared hope for in the days when it all seemed so far away. But to leave the city she loved, her home, her friends...

To leave the man she loved...

It might have taken a while for her to admit it, but it was there: solid and fixed and unshakable. She loved him.

But there was no point pretending he felt the same way. If he wanted to share his life he would want to share it all: the good and the bad. By holding back he was saying she wasn't the one for him. If he could share everything with her the way she had started to with him… If she knew he loved her as much as she loved him…

She shook her head and held back the tears she desperately wanted to shed. In six days she would go to Paris.

End of story.

CHAPTER TWELVE

'New shoes, desserts, nights out; what do they have in common? When there's more than one option available there's nothing worse than having to make a choice.'

THE scenario of the nightmare was no surprise after the events in the convenience store. But the outcome was different.

A shot rang out.

Daniel looked at her. He knew she could see the agony on his face but fought to hide it from her. She staggered forward as he turned, reached for him as he dropped to his knees. Then she was sobbing, their fingers trying to stem the flow of red.

'It's okay,' he said gruffly.

'Don't leave,' she choked.

The pain flayed her soul. As Jo woke up she curled into a ball, hot tears rolling down her cheeks, soaking the pillow. It was the first nightmare she'd ever experienced. How he had got through so many of them…how strong he had to be not to lose his mind… He was so very brave…

She stilled and held her breath, blinking in the darkness, listening to the sounds coming through the wall. The impetus came as a large chunk was torn off her heart. She had to go to him. She didn't have a choice.

Not when he was calling her name.

When Daniel opened the door large watery eyes looked up at him. After tossing tangled tresses of hair over her shoulder, her hands tugged on the belt of a dressing gown. She made a quick study of his face, scowled briefly at his naked chest, then caught her soft lower lip in her teeth and took a breath.

'I can't do this any more,' she confessed in a crackly voice as she shouldered past him. 'We need to talk.'

Talking was the last thing he wanted to do, particularly if it involved sitting still. When something happened Daniel couldn't control, his reaction had always been the same. He had to keep busy. Keep moving. Keep pushing his body until his mind had time to work through it. Lying down sure as hell hadn't helped. Not when he'd been subjected to eight years' worth of failings in one session.

It was tough to believe he could love someone enough to deserve them when he was filled with self-loathing. He frowned as he closed the door. 'You're supposed to be with Liv.'

'I wanted to sleep in my own bed.' Realization crossed her eyes. 'What was the plan if we didn't walk into a stick-up? A night in one of the hotels you stayed in after you got back?'

He scrubbed a palm over his face. 'Jo—'

'Make me coffee.'

'I'm not making you coffee.' He glanced briefly at his watch. 'It's four in the morning.'

'We're talking about this.'

'No, we're not.'

'Yes, we are,' she insisted. 'If you don't talk about it then everything stays locked up in your head and no matter what you do it won't go away. I think you know that.'

He did. He'd said something similar to Jack. But pushing him when she already had him on the run wasn't the right move.

Daniel looked anywhere but into her eyes. Way he saw it, she was right to get as far away from him as possible. It wouldn't take long for a smart woman like her to work out how much more he needed her in his life than she needed him. Since he didn't plan on sticking around for that revelation, he should thank her for beating him to the punch.

'Do you know you were calling my name tonight?' she asked.

He nodded.

'You remember every detail of them when you wake up?'

He nodded again.

After a brief silence, she sighed. 'Go put on a T-shirt. I'll make my own coffee.'

Daniel used it to buy time, splashing water on his face and blinking at the bathroom sink before he dug out a T-shirt. He had to let her say her piece. The break had to be clean. If it wasn't it would take longer to heal. When he returned, she was sitting at the breakfast bar, her gaze fixed on his chest as he walked across the room. He lifted a fist to rub the ache it created, a cavalry charge of sensation thundering across his senses. Coupled with the need to do something physical, his body leapt to attention—cocked, primed and ready for action. But no matter how tempting it was when she looked ruffled and soft and sexy, he couldn't get lost in her any more.

Waiting for him to sit opposite her, she slid a mug across the counter. 'You should drink decaf.'

'Bit pointless drinking coffee if it's not got caffeine.'

She flashed a brief smile. 'I feel the same way. But you should consider it.'

'It won't make a difference.'

'Are the nightmares always worse after your eight-hour coma?'

'Payback.'

Inky lashes swept downward, her gaze studying her mug as she turned it in her hands. 'Did you have the nightmares when you were overseas?'

'Slept like a baby.'

'Explains why you're happy to go back.'

'It's part of it,' he allowed.

'What happened to me in this one?' she asked.

Daniel pressed his mouth into a thin line. Even while she was sitting in front of him, the images remained sickeningly clear in his mind. He honestly didn't know how he could look at her every day, feel the way he did and resist the urge to smother her in the protectiveness she didn't want from him. She would try to soothe and reassure with a whispering touch and softly spoken words but even that wouldn't help.

A man like him should take care of the people he loved. It wasn't supposed to be the other way round.

'We're not talking about it,' he said firmly. 'I know you want me to but I can't.'

Her gaze lifted, her voice soft. 'Yes, you can.'

'No.' He amended the statement, 'I *won't.*'

'Not to me…'

'Not to you…' Looking into her eyes was costing him, but he forced himself to do it without wavering.

She stiffened. 'You were never going to talk to me about this, were you?'

'No.'

The sense of betrayal was palpable. While she'd trusted him with her body and some of her closely guarded memories, he had let go in the bedroom the way she wanted him to but never with anything else.

When her gaze lowered again, Daniel's roved over her hair, long lashes, lush lips and everything in between as if he felt he had to memorize her before she disappeared. She was so damn beautiful, so fragile in body but so strong in spirit.

If she needed him as much as he needed her…if she loved him even half as much as he loved her, then maybe—

She cleared her throat. 'About Paris…'

'What about it?' he said flatly.

'I didn't plan on telling you the way I did.'

'Good to know.'

She shrugged. 'It's been my dream for a long time. I've wanted to go there since I went to work at the magazine and heard about the shortlist they have for the position.' She swiped a strand of tangled hair behind her ear. 'Career-wise it's a golden opportunity.'

Daniel quietly exhaled the breath he hadn't realized he was holding. *Her dream* and he would let her give it up for a *maybe*? He was a selfish son of a—

'I wasn't supposed to go this year,' she continued. 'The girl who was broke her leg and if I'd known—'

'When did you know?' he heard his voice ask.

'Since the day you started texting me.'

'The night you had sex with me for the first time…'

'The night we *made love* for the first time…'

Jo corrected. 'And I swear if you try to make me regret a single—'

'That's what was bothering you.' It made sense to him now. By ambushing him and pushing him on things he didn't want to talk about, she found a way to avoid telling him. Did she know then how much he needed her? How desperate he was to have her?

'Among other things.' She nodded as if confirming his thoughts. 'I wanted to tell you…tried…I just couldn't…'

Do that to him? In case he begged her to stay?

'Before you got on a plane would have been nice,' he said dryly before lifting the mug to his mouth. Since drinking the coffee had the same effect as swallowing acid, he set it back down. 'What else didn't you tell me?'

'Don't do that,' she warned as her gaze lifted. 'I could have left you a Dear Danny letter. Instead I'm here trying to do what you won't: *talk*.'

'If you want to leave, leave.'

'You say that like I think I need your permission.'

A corner of his mouth tugged wryly. 'It's just as well you don't. Didn't hesitate when it came to accepting the offer, did you?' He leaned forward, lowering his voice conspiratorially. 'I'd heard when couples get involved in more than spectacular sex they talk over a decision like that.'

Averting her gaze, she blinked with bewilderment into the middle distance. 'Why do I suddenly feel like this is my fault and nothing to do with you? How did that happen?' She arched a brow at him. 'If you're done playing the jilted lover, maybe you should take a look at the facts and be honest with me. We both said we weren't looking for anything serious. We agreed to see where it took us and that we wouldn't fall in love. Did any of that change for you?'

'Did it change for you?'

'I asked first.' When she realized what she'd said she rolled her eyes. A huff of laughter left her lips, but when she spoke there was a crack in her voice. 'You think this is easy for me? You think I found what happened last night easy? I'm going to Paris. That's not going to change. But if there's something you want to say to me before I go—'

Drawing on every second of training he'd ever been given, Daniel looked her straight in the eye and lied. 'There isn't.'

Time stretched like taffy while she decided whether to believe him. Daniel's protesting heart thundered in his chest while he maintained rigid control over the crippling weakness of his emotions. She'd never know how staggeringly unprepared he had been to fall in love or how far out of his weight he'd been punching when he got involved with her.

'That's that, then.' She stared at him for another moment. For a second he thought he could see her eyes glistening but when she spoke again her voice was flat. 'I've got to go.'

He might have had the strength to leave it at that if she hadn't glanced at him as she stood up. She did it as if she couldn't help herself, a brief frown indicating her annoyance. But that one brief glance into her eyes revealed enough raw vulnerability to tear through Daniel like a knife. It twisted sharply in his chest as he realized what he'd done, or rather *hadn't* done when he should. At the one time she'd needed him anywhere close to as much as he needed her, he'd let her down. With a blinding flash of clarity he realized what she'd wanted from him outside the convenience store. The one simple act it would have taken to avoid what she referred to as a meltdown.

The knowledge broke him so hard and so comprehensively the walls of his resistance collapsed into dust. While he couldn't get down on his knees and beg her to stay or ask her to give up her dream for a maybe, there was one thing he could do.

Across the room in a heartbeat, he flattened his palm on the wood, his voice gravelly. 'I can't leave you like this.'

'You're not the one doing the leaving, remember?' She yanked on the door handle. 'Let me go, Danny.'

'Not till you let it out.' He reached out to draw her to him. 'Come here.'

'No.'

When she took a step back, he took a step forward. She slapped his arms with the backs of her hands, tried to twist free and then pushed him hard in the chest with her palms.

'That's it,' Daniel encouraged. 'Go ahead and hit me if that's what you need to do. I can take it.'

'Why are you doing this?' she choked as she shoved his chest again. 'Why can't you just leave me alone? I *hate* you.'

'I know.'

Her small hands curled into fists against his shoulders. Leaning on them, she lowered her head and pushed her full body weight against him. 'And I *never* cry!'

'Delayed shock,' he reasoned as he circled her body with his arms.

'Let me go,' she pleaded.

'I can't, babe. Not till you let it out.'

Somewhere in the middle of mumbled protests and calling him names, her fists gripped handfuls of his T-shirt. Then she wasn't pushing him away any more. She was holding on tight and leaning on him. It was so close to what he wanted her to do for the rest of their lives Daniel came dangerously close to confessing how he felt, the words forming in his chest instead of his mind.

'I've got you,' he said gruffly.

The first racking sob ripped his heart out. He tightened his arms in response, holding her close as pain reverberated through his body. All she needed was a moment to get it out and then she would be fine. She would rediscover the joy she found in life, light up from inside the way he loved best and at least while she was in France, living her dream, Daniel would know she was happy.

So he held her while an eight-year-old mourned her mother and a fourteen-year-old showed how scared she had been every time a difficult bar owner got in her face. He smoothed silky hair while the eighteen-year-old faced her first night without a roof over her head and watched a boy she knew bleed to death in the arms of a female cop who would become her best friend.

He remained silent and solid; standing guard over her so the world would never know she had a moment of weakness after a lifetime of being strong. It was their secret. One he would keep for her until the day he died.

'Tell me to stay,' she whispered in a voice so low and muffled he had to strain to hear it.

'I can't do that,' he whispered back.

If she wanted to stay he wouldn't have to tell her. Part of the reason he loved her so much was because she was a born fighter. She might not believe it in her weakened state but his Jo was fearless in the face of adversity. She reached out and grabbed what she wanted with both hands. It was the final confirmation Daniel needed that he wasn't it. Not for her.

Gradually she regained control. 'I'm okay now,' she said against his chest. Leaning back, she swiped her cheeks. 'Might need a tissue, but apart from that...'

'You can use my T-shirt,' Daniel volunteered roughly.

She smiled tremulously. 'Shut up.'

When she looked up at him, as hard as it was to take, he knew she was going to be fine without him. A long enough break from him to catch up on her sleep, the first glimpse she got of her dream and she would bounce right back—probably a lot faster than he would. Unable to resist, he lowered his head for a soft, slow kiss; one intended to show her how he felt when he still couldn't say the words.

He loved her—he always would—and if she ever needed a chest to cry on all she had to do was come find him and he'd be there.

As their lips parted her fingertips whispered over his jaw, head leaning into the palm that framed her face.

He looked into her eyes. 'Go grab your dream, babe.'

'You try and get rid of a few,' she replied with a small, wavering smile as she lowered her hand to his chest.

'I will,' he promised.

When she dropped her arm and stepped around him, Daniel stayed where he was, unable to watch her leave.

CHAPTER THIRTEEN

'The mark of a best friend is someone who will tell you yes, your ass does look big in those jeans. It may be tough to admit but sometimes we all need an intervention.'

Attending Sunday lunch with the Brannigans might not have been the best idea she ever had. Not when pretending she was fine and looking forward to Paris was wearing her mask thin.

Surrounded by people who looked like Danny in a house filled with pictures of him didn't help any more than the work she'd used to fill the days before she left. But at least now she knew why he had been so easy to avoid. According to his siblings he had an EMT cert due for renewal; one that required he immediately jump on an empty spot in an available course.

Jo knew she should be grateful when there was a very good chance seeing him again would have resulted in the same plea she'd made last time.

But she ached for another glimpse of him in the same way her chest ached if she held her breath for too long. She missed him so much the pain was debilitating.

She missed the little leap of anticipation her pulse made when her phone said she had a text or there was a knock on her door. She missed the kiss that suggested the time he'd spent away from her was filled with thoughts of getting her naked again. She missed the calmness on his face when he slept in bed beside her; how it smoothed out the creases at the corners of his eyes. She missed his clean masculine scent, the heat of his touch, the punch of his infamous smile, the rumble of his voice and the sound of his laughter... She even missed arguing with him at the times he bugged her most. She just missed him.

'Who's for cheesecake?' his mother asked.

Since the traditional gathering for Sunday lunch had been turned into a 'Bon Voyage' party, Jo pinned yet another false smile into place. 'Me, please.'

Turning to hand over the pile of dessert plates to Liv in the seat beside her, she saw her friend still. 'You okay?'

'Forgive me,' she whispered as she looked into Jo's eyes and took the plates.

'What for?'

The sound of a door slam was followed by a familiar deep voice. 'I know I'm late. Not my fault. Took half of Ed Marks' shift when his wife went into labour and at the end of it some idiot flipped over a car avoiding a cat.'

Jo's breath caught. Oh, she was *so* not ready for this. She couldn't sit there, *opposite him*, and pretend she was fine.

'Your plate is in the oven,' his mother called. 'It's hot, so use a cloth.'

Frozen in place, gaze glued to the table in front of her, Jo wondered if she looked as shocked as she felt. Her cheeks felt as if they were on fire.

'How do you flip over a car avoiding a cat?' Tyler asked from further down the table.

'Beats me,' Daniel's voice said as he got closer.

By the time Jo saw his waist appear she was pretty sure she was having a panic attack. She checked for the symptoms. Racing pulse, lack of oxygen, light head, shaking hands… She stifled a burst of semi-hysterical laughter.

Just as well there was a fully re-certified EMT in the room, wasn't it?

'Can't blame the driver for a series of freak events.' He dropped the plate into his place and shook his hand.

'I said the plate was hot,' his mother said as he kissed her cheek. 'Boy or girl?'

'Don't know yet.' He pulled out his chair. 'Said I'd be happy with a Danielle or a Daniel… So what's the big family emergency I had to…?'

As his voice trailed off if felt as if the whole room went silent. Jo continued staring at the table, her heart beating so loud she was surprised no one could hear it. This was *not happening* and she was not going to cry even if it felt as if she'd sprung a damn leak over the last few days.

As he sat down opposite her she thought about looking at him and knew she couldn't do it. It had been difficult enough leaving him last time without telling him how she felt. She didn't think she could do it twice.

'Jo?'

Her gaze jumped sharply to the left where a cheesecake was waiting on a serving dish. She couldn't eat that. She'd choke.

'I don't think… I'm not…' Pressing her lips together, she sucked in a breath through her nose and swallowed hard before looking at Daniel's mother. 'Packing still…blog to write…' She flashed a smile as she jerked a thumb over her shoulder. 'I should…' She nodded. Pushing her chair back, she stood up and ducked down to kiss a cheek. 'Thanks for lunch.'

Practically running into the hall, she yanked her coat from the rack and left. It was official: she would have to live in France for the rest of her days.

As she stormed down the path and argued with the latch on the gate, she started to get angry at him for the first time since he'd let her walk away. Why couldn't he have left things the way they were when she hated him? She'd been *comfortable* hating him. He had no business making her fall in love with him, and what the hell was with the whole tenderness thing when her heart had been breaking? She swung open the gate. Of all the inconsiderate, unforgivable, inconceivably hurtful things he could possibly have done—

'Why aren't you in Paris?'

She swung around when she heard the deep rumble of his voice, anger giving her the strength she needed to face him. 'Did you know I'd be here?'

'Did it *look* like I knew?'

'I don't know. I couldn't look at you!'

He frowned at her, looking every bit as angry as she felt. 'Somewhat ironic considering I couldn't keep my eyes off you.'

Jo glanced at the house, realization dawning when she saw a twitching curtain at a window. 'Were we just ambushed?'

'I thought you'd met my family,' he said dryly. 'Didn't I mention how much they love to stage an intervention?'

'Staging an intervention suggests this is a problem which can be fixed,' she snapped at him. 'Since you made it obvious it can't you can go back in there and explain why.'

Daniel's eyes narrowed. 'What happened to equal terms and not being made out to be a victim of seduction?'

'You want to tell them I seduced you, go right ahead, but if you think for a single second I'm going to let them look at me like some poor broken-hearted sap who was foolish enough to fall in—' She slapped a hand over her mouth, her eyes widening with horror.

Angling his head, Daniel looked at her from the corner of his eye and took an ominous step forward, his voice low. 'You want to finish that sentence for me?'

Jo dropped her arm to her side and glared at him. 'How about you hold your breath while you wait? And don't think I haven't figured out another of your lies, Daniel Brannigan. I *knew* you had a problem with me being here on a Sunday. The second you thought I was gone you were back in that chair.'

He stilled and rocked back on his heels. His gaze searched the air for a moment as he crossed his jaw and then he looked her straight in the eye. 'I got to give it to my family—their timing is excellent. Having carried this around for a week I'm ready to offload and it's not like either of us was going to make the first move this time, was it?' He took a short breath. 'You want to know the problem? For five and a half years you were a giant pain in my ass. There were times I used to wish you would get hit by a cab or a piano would fall on you.'

'That's so sweet.' She smirked.

He took a measured step forward, the predatory gleam in his eyes making her feel as if he were a hunter and she were the prey. 'Then you start dressing like every guy's ideal cross between a librarian and a stripper.'

She gasped. 'I have *never* dressed like a stripper!'

'One word: *boots*. And did it sound like a complaint?' He took another measured step forward. 'You make me crazier than any woman I've ever known. You're so confident and independent you make it virtually impossible for a guy to figure out where he's supposed to fit into your life.'

She popped her fists onto her hips and angled her chin. 'He could try not letting me leave. It's a lot easier to fit into someone's life if they're on the same continent.'

'You said it was your dream.'

'Dreams *change*.'

'I know.'

She faltered. 'Are you telling me they're gone?'

He stilled a couple of feet away from her. 'Oh, I'm sure they'll be back. But it turns out they're less frequent when I have a bigger problem to deal with.'

'Feel free to not talk about that either.'

'I'm over here trying to tell you I'm in love with you and you'd still prefer to fight with me? Okay.' He shook his head and folded his arms. 'What do you want to know? Should I start at the beginning? First nightmare was my dad having his heart attack. I couldn't resuscitate him.'

'You weren't here when he died.' Jo frowned. 'Liv said he was on his own.'

'He was.' Daniel nodded. 'He died a couple of hours after I left. I came home on leave to tell him I was staying in the Marines, he reminded me he'd agreed to give his consent on the proviso I would come back and join the family business. Didn't mention he wanted me here 'cos he was sick, but after an hour of yelling at me about loyalty, duty, responsibility and not reacting particularly well to the fact Uncle Sam had taught me not to flinch under fire, I thanked him for his support over the years and walked out.'

The information made her frown. 'How does that make his death your fault?'

Pressing his mouth into a thin line, his shoulders dropped in a very visible hint of the weight he'd carried for so long. 'You need more, here goes. Next up was Liv—I was standing in the station the night she walked in covered in blood. At the time I thought it was hers—she wouldn't let me near her, said she was evidence. Brannigans watch over each other: my dad did it for Johnnie,

Johnnie did it for Reid and so on till it was my turn with Liv. I figured she was tough, she knew what she was getting into—she didn't need my help. I was *wrong*.'

Since Jo knew more about the events of that night than he did, she had to clear her throat before she could speak. 'That wasn't your fault any more than Aiden's death was Liv's.'

He ignored her. 'The two more I was yelling about that night? Inches of space I needed to put pressure on an artery. Guy was trapped under a wall. He died.'

Her gaze immediately lowered to the hand he had scraped on a wall, the pieces falling into place. 'They're all the people you've lost or came close to losing. You torture yourself even though you know it wasn't your fault.'

'It's my job to save lives—to be there when people need me. No matter how I try I keep messing that up.'

When her gaze lifted, for the first time Jo could see through the shadows in his eyes to the pain; the starkness of it almost breaking her in two. 'You were there for me,' she told him in a voice thick with emotion. 'Doesn't that count?'

'Except I wasn't, was I?' His deep voice was

rougher than she'd ever heard it before. 'The one time you needed me to be there I let you down.'

Jo searched his eyes, frowning with confusion. 'You threw yourself in front of a gun for me. I've never been as scared as I was when you did that. I tried to find the words to tell you but I couldn't. If you'd died saving me, if I'd *lost you*...'

When he looked at her with enough yearning to take her breath away, she blinked. 'Wait a minute...what did you say?'

He pushed his hands into the pockets of his jeans. 'The one time you needed—'

'No.' She made a jumping motion with her forefinger. 'Go back further...' A sudden flare of hope made her heart falter and skip a beat. 'Did you say you're in love with me?'

The warmth in his eyes seemed to smooth the grimness from his face, making him look younger and unbelievably vulnerable. 'Was beginning to wonder if you'd noticed...'

Jo's faltering heart leapt, did handsprings and swelled to proportions that made it feel as if it couldn't be contained in her chest. 'If you're in love with me, then why did you let me leave, you idiot?' Realization dawned. 'You were scared... *of me*?' She took a step closer and looked deeper into his eyes, searching for answers, her voice filled with wonder when she found them. 'No, not of me—of how you felt about me… But I asked if you wanted to tell me anything and—'

He shifted his weight from one foot to the other in a move she found impossibly endearing. 'I'm not the kind of guy who's gonna read you poetry or wear his heart on his sleeve. I think you know that by now. When it comes to how I feel the only way I can show it is by—'

'Protecting the people you love and looking after them.'

'Yes.'

'The things I told you I didn't want from you…'

His mouth tugged wryly. 'Yes.'

'So you were afraid to tell me you needed me because you didn't think I felt the same way?'

He let out a long breath. 'I'm always going to need you more than you need me.'

'You are *so* competitive.' Jo shook her head, the move immediately contradicted by the smile blossoming on her lips. She shrugged a shoulder a little self-consciously. 'I know I may have given the impression I don't need you but I thought you knew me better by now. I don't need you to protect me from every bump in life. But that doesn't mean there aren't times… I've needed you for longer than… I guess I was so focused on other things… Maybe I never knew…but I do now…'

Daniel released a small smile. 'You know you've been doing that a lot this last while.'

'Losing the ability to speak?' She puffed a soft burst of laughter. 'Yeah, I'd noticed that. I blame you.'

'Nothing new there, then.'

'Oh, there's something new,' she whispered.

As if some kind of shutter had been lowered, her feelings showed clearly in her eyes for the first time. Daniel's hunger for her entwined with a depth of tenderness that shook him to the very foundation of who he'd thought he was. The connection he felt to her in response to her need was a visceral tug. It drew him forward and pulled him in. He took his hands out of his pockets as he stepped forward.

She took a stuttered breath when he was close enough to drag a knuckle along the skin of her cheek, her hand shaking as it flattened on his chest, directly above his pounding heart. Her throat convulsed before she spoke. 'You're wrong to think I don't need you, Danny. I needed you the day we met but I was too scared to admit it. What we have now was a dream too far out of my reach then, so I told myself I didn't want it.'

He threaded his fingers into silky hair as he framed her face. 'Your dream involved a guy who could feed you one of the worst lines you'd ever heard?'

Jo shook her head. 'That's not when we met.'

'What?'

'You think we met that fourth of July weekend. We didn't. We met two months before that.'

Daniel frowned. 'I'd have remembered.'

'Would you?' She lifted her brows and smiled tremulously. 'I was no one then.'

'You've never been no one,' he said firmly.

'I was invisible to most of the world; though in fairness that was partly my fault.' She blinked and took a deep breath. 'Make yourself invisible and you can fall between the cracks in the system. That worked for me for a long time. But you wouldn't believe how badly you want to be seen when you're homeless. The number of people who will walk past you without ever looking you in the eye...' When her voice wavered she took another short breath. 'Liv was the first. Then one day she was there with her partner talking to me when another squad car pulled up across the street and you got out.'

Daniel frantically searched his normally reliable memory as inky lashes lowered and she focused on the hand resting on his chest.

'You started talking to Liv, exchanged a few jokes with her partner—'

'Tell me I looked at you,' he rasped.

Her gaze lifted, shimmering with deeply felt emotion. 'Oh, you did something much worse. You looked straight into my eyes and smiled at me.' She blinked back tears. 'It was like…the sun coming out from behind a cloud or…*stardust*. I'd never seen anything like it before. When you took it away…when you left…' She cleared her throat and shrugged. 'For a second you had turned a graduate of the school of hard knocks into some starry-eyed, weak-at-the-knees daydreamer and I *hated you* for that. Because when you were gone and I wasn't blinded by that infamous smile of yours I had to open my eyes again.'

Daniel hadn't known it was possible to love someone the way he loved her. He wished he had been ready for her back then, that it hadn't taken so long to see what was right in front of him. Most of all he wished he'd been brave enough to take a chance on what he could have missed if the people who loved them hadn't banged their stubborn heads together. But if she'd fallen in love with him, unworthy as he was, he couldn't be too far beyond redemption to turn things around.

'Starry-eyed dreamers didn't survive in the world I lived in then,' she explained in her softest voice. 'So I toughened up, got twice as hard and the next time you saw me you didn't stand a chance.'

When the memory came to him, Daniel closed his eyes for a second. 'Did you have a really dumb hat?'

She blinked at him. 'What?'

The image was still foggy. 'It had ears.'

'Floppy dog ears.' She nodded as if he were insane to think anything else. 'I had three but it was my favourite. They were winter ski-hats a store donated to charity.'

Daniel smiled indulgently as he tucked a strand of hair behind her ear. 'It was *May*.'

'A person loses something like seventy per cent of their body heat through their head so I figured at night...' She bit down on her lower lip. 'You remember.'

'I asked Liv about you.' He wrapped an arm

around her waist and drew her to him. 'Thought you were under age… You looked about sixteen with those braids in.'

'Nope, eighteen. I can't believe you remember.'

Lowering his head, he breathed in lavender shampoo, a deep-seated sense of contentment washing over him. 'You didn't look like that next time I saw you…'

'Liv took me for my first girly make-over.'

Nudging the tip of his nose into her fringe, he pressed a light kiss to her temple, his mouth moving against her skin as he confessed, 'You deserved better than that line. You were right to cut me down the way you did.'

'It was a really bad line,' she agreed as she hooked a thumb into one of the belt loops of his jeans. 'But you didn't deserve my response, Danny. I started a five-and-a-half-year war between us when we could have been doing this…'

'No,' he disagreed. 'You were eighteen. I was twenty-four. Six years made a bigger difference then. But even if it hadn't we weren't ready for this. While you were stepping out into the world and claiming a corner of it, I'd already started to retreat.' Leaning back, he used a thumb beneath her chin to lift it and looked into her mesmerizing eyes. 'I'm not gonna find talking about the night-mares easy, babe. But I'm willing to try. You'll have to work with me on that and a couple of other things. Being less protective won't be easy either and I know we'll argue about that. I can be—'

'Oh, I *know*. But so can I…' She silenced him with a soft, all-too-brief kiss. 'Still fell in love, didn't we?'

'You better be sure about that,' he warned. ''Cos once you say you're mine, that's it. We're gonna have to work at this every day but—'

'We will.' Love glowed from her eyes, lighting her up like a beacon. 'I love you, Danny. Even when I wanted to I couldn't make it go away. I don't want it to now. So if you need me to say it—yes, I'm yours.' She sighed, her gaze lowering. 'I can't get out of Paris…'

'I don't want you to, babe.' Daniel shook his head, his palm smoothing over her hair. 'The last few days I've run over dozens of different ways we could have made this work if you loved me the way I love you. How long will you be gone?'

'Three months.' She grimaced.

'Half a tour of duty…' He smiled when she looked at him. 'Way I see it, you going overseas is no different. You'd wait for me, right?'

She nodded. 'Yes.'

'Well, then, look at it this way—we get more opportunities for phone sex and conjugal visits...'

'I do fly home for Liv's wedding next month,' she pouted.

'I reckon I can book some time off either side of that for a couple of long weekends in Paris.' He lowered his head. 'How hot do you think I can make you for me before I get there?'

'Pretty hot.' She smiled as her chin lifted. 'If you pick the right words...'

'I'll buy a dictionary.'

'Did I mention the reason I'm still here is because of an air traffic controller thing? Or ground crew... I forget now...' she mumbled against his mouth.

'Tell them I said thanks.' He angled his head. 'How long have we got?'

'Two days...'

Her lips parted when he kissed her; the sweet taste of her breath caught on his tongue. His fingers slid deeper into her hair, palm cupping the back of her head as he deepened the kiss and the arm around her waist brought her closer. Perfect breasts crushed against his chest, fine-boned hands gripped a shoulder and the back of his neck.

They could pack a lot into two days. It was sure as hell a challenge he was willing to accept. But before he did…

He leaned back and looked down at heavy-lidded eyes and kiss-swollen lips. 'They're at the window, aren't they?'

Jo glanced sideways and chuckled. 'Yes.'

'Want to see how fast I can make them move?' He grinned. 'You stay here. I'll be right back. Watch the window.'

As he turned and jogged towards the house, Jo looked at the window and laughed. Biting down on her lip, she gently swung her skirt while she waited for him to come back. She'd never been so happy. Danny loved her. He. Loved. Her. How could she have been so afraid of something so wonderful? Everything was so clear to her now, as if a veil of fear had been removed from her eyes. She should have viewed love the same way she viewed life and the moments of fun she was so addicted to. Grabbing hold of the good things and holding on tight made the tough stuff easier to take. Together they could face anything, even if it was the weaknesses within themselves. Her pulse sang loudly with a mixture of love, lust and joyous laughter when he returned and finally Jo could hear what it was saying. It had been singing to him all along. Two words, repeated over and over again in elated recognition.

It's you: he was her guy.

'Miss me?'

'Yes,' she answered without hesitation.

'Just so you know. If I ever thought I'd be doing this, I didn't picture it with an audience.' He took a deep, satisfied breath and smiled. 'But since one of them brought you into my life and the rest of them kept you here until I was ready for you, it seems kinda appropriate.'

Jo smiled back at him. 'What are you talking about?'

'This.'

She gasped as he lowered to one knee. 'Danny, you don't have to do that.'

His brows lifted. 'You think I'm letting you go to Paris without everyone knowing you're mine?'

'I'm coming back.'

'And when you do we plan on spending the rest of our lives together, right?'

'Yes.'

He waved the small box in his hand. 'That's usually what one of these says to the world.'

'You bought a ring?' Her eyes widened.

'Do you think you could shut up for a minute?' She pressed her lips together. 'Mmm-hmm.'

When he spoke again his deep rough voice was laced with heartfelt sincerity. 'Jorja Elizabeth Dawson. You've been an adopted member of this family for a long time. I want to make it official by giving you my name. I love you, Jo. Will you...' he smiled his infamous smile '...marry me?'

Jo tried loosening her throat to speak.

'This is traditionally where you give me an answer,' he hinted heavily.

When she nodded frantically in reply, it shook the word loose. 'Yes.' She framed his gorgeous face with her hands and leaned down to kiss him. 'Yes, yes, yes.'

Large hands lifted to her waist, squeezing tight as he pushed to his feet and her arms moved to circle his neck. It felt as if they couldn't hold on to each other tight enough, even when he crushed her to him and lifted her off her feet. After swinging her feet from side to side, he set her down and opened the box. 'For the record, I did look at rings when I was running through ways of making this work. Did it while wearing tactical gear, so didn't take *any* flack from the rest of the team. Then I remembered this.' He took the ring out and reached for her hand. 'You can thank Grandma Brannigan and the fact I was her favourite grandson after I rescued her cat from a tree when I was seven. Might need to get it resized but...' He stared at her finger as it slipped into place. *'Maybe not...'*

Jo smiled at the winking sapphire, the same blue as his eyes when they darkened and she knew he wanted her. 'It fits.'

'Guess you were meant to have it, then, weren't you?'

She beamed when he looked at her.

'You ready to go back in? Sooner we finish lunch, the more time we can spend in bed before you leave.'

'I'm a course ahead of you,' she pointed out smugly as their fingers threaded together. 'Eat fast.'

A suspicious silence met them in the hall as Danny took her coat and hung it on the rack. It was just as quiet in the dining room when they stepped into it hand in hand. When Danny looked down at her from the corner of his eye she grinned. Who did their family think they were kidding? It was only as they approached the table emotion started to get the better of her. When he reached for her chair, his mother broke the silence.

'Everyone move round. Give Jo her place beside Danny.'

Long fingers squeezed hers as everyone moved and he led her around the table. She'd watched it happen with Johnnie's wife and when Liv brought Blake home, but Jo had never thought one day the gesture would be made for her. It was almost too much. Suddenly she belonged in a way she never had anywhere else. Sitting by the man she was going to spend the rest of her life with, she looked at the faces of the people she loved as they acted as if nothing unusual had happened.

She held up pretty well until she got to Liv, but when she did there was no stopping the tears. *Thank you*, she mouthed.

Liv's eyes shimmered, a hand waving in front of her body until Blake placed a napkin in it.

When Jo looked at Danny, he shook his head and glared at his sister. 'Stop making my fiancée cry.'

It was all it took to fill the room with sound.

'Missed your chance, Ty.'

'Not over till the pretty lady says, "I do."'

'I'm not wearing a monkey suit twice in one year.'

'You'll do as you're told, Reid Brannigan.'

Danny leaned in for a quick kiss before fending off his mother's offer to reheat his food, leaving Jo to sigh happily as she was handed a slice of cheesecake. Turned out the ideal guy *had* moved in across the hall from her.

Who knew?

* * * * *

Mills & Boon® Large Print
August 2012

A DEAL AT THE ALTAR
Lynne Graham

RETURN OF THE MORALIS WIFE
Jacqueline Baird

GIANNI'S PRIDE
Kim Lawrence

UNDONE BY HIS TOUCH
Annie West

THE CATTLE KING'S BRIDE
Margaret Way

NEW YORK'S FINEST REBEL
Trish Wylie

THE MAN WHO SAW HER BEAUTY
Michelle Douglas

THE LAST REAL COWBOY
Donna Alward

THE LEGEND OF DE MARCO
Abby Green

STEPPING OUT OF THE SHADOWS
Robyn Donald

DESERVING OF HIS DIAMONDS?
Melanie Milburne

Mills & Boon® Large Print

September 2012

A VOW OF OBLIGATION
Lynne Graham

DEFYING DRAKON
Carole Mortimer

PLAYING THE GREEK'S GAME
Sharon Kendrick

ONE NIGHT IN PARADISE
Maisey Yates

VALTIERI'S BRIDE
Caroline Anderson

THE NANNY WHO KISSED HER BOSS
Barbara McMahon

FALLING FOR MR MYSTERIOUS
Barbara Hannay

THE LAST WOMAN HE'D EVER DATE
Liz Fielding

HIS MAJESTY'S MISTAKE
Jane Porter

DUTY AND THE BEAST
Trish Morey

THE DARKEST OF SECRETS
Kate Hewitt